MW00617737

To Mary;
a very fine and wonderful
person to know.
Sincerely;
Yvonne A. Ford

Keep Hope Alive

by

Yvonne A. Ford

DORRANCE PUBLISHING CO., INC.
PITTSBURGH, PENNSYLVANIA 15222

The contents of this work including, but not limited to, the accuracy of events, people, and places depicted; opinions expressed; permission to use previously published materials included; and any advice given or actions advocated are solely the responsibility of the author, who assumes all liability for said work and indemnifies the publisher against any claims stemming from publication of the work.

All Rights Reserved
Copyright © 2012 by Yvonne A. Ford

No part of this book may be reproduced or transmitted, downloaded, distributed, reverse engineered, or stored in or introduced into any information storage and retrieval system, in any form or by any means, including photocopying and recording, whether electronic or mechanical, now known or hereinafter invented without permission in writing from the publisher.

Dorrance Publishing Co., Inc.
701 Smithfield Street
Pittsburgh, PA 15222
Visit our website at www.dorrancebookstore.com

ISBN: 978-1-4349-1490-3
eISBN: 978-1-4349-1408-8

I wish to dedicate my book to Vivian Ford, my beloved sister and best friend. She was always my greatest cheerleader and went to her grave believing in the completion and success of
Keep Hope Alive.
Vivian was a wonderful daughter, sister, aunt, mother, and grandmother. She brought out the best in all of us, especially me. Thank you, little sister, for helping make my dream come true.

Keep Hope Alive chronicles life on a large plantation in Tennessee. There are lots of strange twists and unexpected turns.

One slave family stands out throughout the entire book. Faith, courage, and perseverance sustained them during those dark, perilous times.

Freedom allows them to attain heights they dared not even pray for. This story is compelling, captivating, and uplifting.

Jesse Monroe Ferguson was the proud owner and czar of a 2,000-acre plantation in Tennessee with over two hundred slaves. He is a brilliant businessman who never suspected that his downfall was eminent.

Massa Ferguson was a tall, thick man without an ounce of fat. His full head of dark hair was thick and wavy. He spoke in a loud booming voice that commanded attention.

Ferguson was rich, powerful, and ruthless. His privileged life could not be better.

Miz Lucinda Marie Ferguson was the mistress of Tall Oaks and the wife of J.M. Ferguson. She was indeed the queen of the empire that her husband created. She was a well educated and beautiful Southern belle. Miz Lucinda was a tall, stately, blond who loved beautiful clothes, elegant furniture, and elaborate dinner parties. Her father was a very wealthy tobacco plantation owner. Lucinda Marie was born with a silver spoon in her mouth. She went from rich to richer when she got married. Her home and plantation were among the largest in the county. The ambience of the mansion was as natural to her as breathing. From all outward appearances, she was as sweet as her syrupy Southern accent.

Dixon Ferguson was Massa Ferguson's right hand person and best slave. He was small-boned, short, but a very muscular man. One leg appeared to be shorter than the other, causing him to rock from side to side, swinging the shorter leg to the opposite side to regain his balance. Dixon was in charge of the livery stable. This was a job he was born into. He learned this from his father. Dixon was also in charge of the fancy carriages and buggies, and the only driver for Massa Ferguson and Miz Lucinda. He was an inventor, as well as a keeper and trainer of the race-horses. Of all the slaves on the plantation, not one was a greater asset than Dixon. He never caused a moment's trouble, was dedicated, hardworking, and silent. He was loyal and humble, but there was another side to him...

Annabelle Ferguson, the wife of Dixon, and Miz Ferguson's favorite slave, maid, and personal caretaker, was the downstairs maid. She was a tall, mulatto (half black, half white), confident, efficient, and the best cleaner in all of Tennessee. Absolutely, no one in the world had as much energy as Annabelle. She treated Miz Ferguson as if she were a rare and valuable china doll. She coifed her hair, took great pains with her clothes, tends to the downstairs, and does any and everything that makes Miz Ferguson happy. Annabelle was also the plantation's holistic healer. She delivered a passel of strong, healthy slave babies every year. She can treat sprains, cuts, colds, and whatever ails the slaves. She also treats all the farm animals if they are sick. A true healer she was. These secrets were brought from Africa by her female ancestors, passed down, and, with each generation, improved upon. Annabelle's voice was like liquid. She was soft-spoken, kind, obedient, and loyal.

Yancy Ferguson was the son of Dixon and Annabelle, their firstborn. There was not a smarter or better behaved child on the entire plantation. He was tall for his age, the spitting image of his mother, and quiet like both of his parents. His job was to lend a hand to his father and learn from him. Yancy helps clean the barns, assist with the horses, the carriages, the buggies, and with many other chores. He also shines and helps repair Massa's boots and shoes. Even at a young age, he was already as cunning as his father. Yancy never made eye contact with anyone on the plantation, except his family, fearing that someone will see the intelligence in his eyes, or see all the way into his determined soul.

Dixiebelle Ferguson was the second child of Dixon and Annabelle. She was tall like her mother, but small-boned and fine-featured like her father. From a very young age, Dixiebelle watched, helped, and learned from her mother. She and her mother plant, tend, harvest, and dry herbs grown on the plantation, which were used for all manner of medicines, elixirs, and cure-alls. They even made cosmetics and smell good potions.

Hawthorne, known as the "Basin," was located in the center of the state of Tennessee, where the soil was rich and black. Everything grew in great profusion between the warm, rich soil and free labor force…commonly referred to as slaves.

The "Basin" was the most desirable land to own in the state. Whether you raise cotton, tobacco, or just a large vegetable garden, you can raise two bumper crops a season. Of course, the land sells for an absolute premium.

Fortunately, the growing season was so long, and the field hands have very little down time. By the time you harvest the last crop, it was time to prepare for the next season.

The Southern plantation owner, as a general rule, was rich, arrogant, and ruthless, to say the least. To own people—human flesh—was simply a way of life to these "black-hearted" slave owners.

This book is an incredible, heart-wrenching story about "keeping hope alive" no matter how insufferable the conditions are. This is a saga, a journey, an evolution recorded by the personal maid to the mistress of Tall Oaks Plantation, Annabelle Ferguson.

Chapter One

It was in the year of 1853, late fall. This year was no different from any other. The backbreaking work was never really finished, just a cycle, year after year. Here at Tall Oaks Plantation, the last of the harvesting was finished; even the cotton bolls had been pulled. Now was the time of the year to make certain that enough food and goods had been stored up for the winter. The female slaves made lye soap for cleaning and milder perfumed soaps for use in the big house. The fruit had been picked and made into jellies and preserves, and canned and stored down in the dark, cool cellar that ran the length of the mansion. There were so many delicious varieties: sand plum, grape, apricot, strawberry, peach, pear, and, of course, watermelon rind.

There were fresh meats of all kinds in the ice cave: fishes, chickens, turkeys, and so forth. It was packed full with delicious frozen meats—something unheard of back then in Tennessee.

By this time of the year, the smokehouse was filled to the brim with meats from the hog butchering. The salted sides of hogs hang from the smokehouse ceiling. The storehouses were bulging.

Wheat was grown for use in the plantation for flour to make bread, pasta, and cakes, and also for export. The largest and most profitable crop was tobacco. It was shipped all over the world, mainly from the ports in New Orleans.

Tall Oaks was complete within itself, every square foot of it. The owner, J.M. Ferguson, was a brilliant businessman. His entire operation was run on a code of excellence. Each and every job and every chore had to be done in an excellent manner, not just good. No exceptions were allowed.

Massa Ferguson prided himself on owning a unique and remarkable piece of heaven on earth. His empire was progressive, productive, and very profitable. This was all due to his genius…or so he thought.

His 200 slaves, give or take a few, were taught and trained by him or his white overseer, Bo. They were experts in each and every one of their endeavors. This was tantamount to Tall Oaks' success.

There were cobblers on the plantation who make long wearing, well fitting, comfortable shoes for everyone on the place. They use the tanned hides of the cattle raised right there at Tall Oaks.

There were seamstresses who make all the slaves' clothes, from work clothes to Sunday clothes. Most work clothing was white to reflect the sun, with bright headscarves for the women to cover their heads. Fine silk and brocade draperies were also made for the big house. They also made intricate coverlets, embroidered tablecloths, and baby clothes. All work was done fast, efficiently, and expertly with that indomitable code of excellence.

The master brick masons were adept at laying the magnificent, meandering brick road that led up the hill to the big house. On a trip to New Orleans, Massa Ferguson hired two very outstanding bricklayers right off their jobs. They were paid to teach several of his slaves to do the quality and style of work J.M. observed them doing. For the three months they were working and teaching, the group constructed tiered flowerbeds across the front and back of the huge house. Paved walkways lead out to the various outhouses on the property. Sure cuts down on tracking dirt, grass, leaves, etc., inside. What a brilliant idea!

Enough fruit and vegetables were grown by the slaves to supply the owners and all the 200 plus slaves with full bellies, even in the winter months. Female slaves had pickled, dried, and stored food during all the growing season. In the winter months, they quilt and do handwork.

There were many unique activities going on at Tall Oaks. Money kept pouring in. Tennessee walkers and racehorses were bred, groomed, and trained right on the Tall Oaks' grounds. The racehorses were later sold to businessmen in Kentucky, and the walkers were purchased far and wide. They were much sought after.

Several years ago, Dixon said to his son Yancy, "You is to become the horse trainer and expert on horses. I will teach you." And so he did. It was not long before he could ride correctly, train, and even talk to the horses.

Massa Ferguson enjoyed watching Yancy work with his prized horses. "Boy, you make me proud. No one has ever handled these beasts like you do. Keep up the good work."

Yancy would say, "Sho will Massa, thank you much, Sir. Love your horses."

And with a big smile, he would walk or ride away. Thinking all the time, *Are you stupid? Can you not feel or see my hatred?*

A special formula was devised by Dixon, the slave in charge of the horses. This concoction made the horses' coats silky, shiny, and beautiful. It also made their bones strong, and developed better wind capacity in their lungs. This was especially useful for the racehorses.

Inventors abound at Tall Oaks. Once again, Dixon came up with the first ice crusher and even an ice cave. Of course, all inventions were patented and sold by the Massa. These inventions further fatten his coffers.

Dixon's wife, Annabelle, grew her own herbs and could heal a horse or a slave. (In her special garden, she also grew yarrow for fever, pokeberry for arthritis, wild garlic and shod for colds, and cherry bark for coughs, just to mention a few.)

Every year, Annabelle was able to deliver a passel of strong, healthy black babies. She even provided all of the prenatal care for the expectant mothers. She prescribed them with elixirs during pregnancy, and pain medication during and after birth. Both the babies and the mothers thrived. She was worth her weight in gold to Massa Ferguson.

Absolutely, no one at Tall Oaks was ever starved or beaten. Massa said, "A slave who has to be beaten isn't worth his salt. If you injure a slave by beating him, he is no good to me, and certainly isn't any good to anyone else, so you sell him immediately." Massa Ferguson will sell a slave at the drop of a hat. He would not hesitate to break up a family because of a troublesome member of his team. Tall Oaks ran like a well-oiled machine.

If for some reason, Massa Ferguson inadvertently selected or bought a slave who was incapable of being trained to his level of excellence, he was sold immediately.

Ferguson prided himself on being an excellent judge of slave mentality.

On the other hand, if a new member of his slave team was stubborn, uncooperative, and just plain lazy, he was sold fast! Quickly, he was discarded as not suitable for his master plan. Perfection was everything.

There were many interesting things about the natural lay of the land. First of all, the large lake was fed by numerous underground springs and was full of several kinds of delicious fishes: croppie, rainbow trout, and catfish. Natural springs were scattered about the property. The field hands did not have to venture far to get a refreshing cool drink. That in itself was a blessing.

Over and over, during the day, you would hear one of the hot, sweaty field hands yell, "Water! Water!" One of the many small children nearby would quickly fetch the cool refreshing water. The children were delighted to help out. There was still plenty of time to play.

Located just outside the detached kitchen was a fairly large, round, deep hole. It was a holding pool for live fish. The cook simply had to take a net and gather a batch of fish to fry for dinner at a moment's notice.

Nellie, the head cook, had endeared herself to the Massa for life. After each meal she prepared when he was home, he never failed to walk down to the detached kitchen and say in his booming voice, "Nellie, you are the best cook in the land. That meal was fit for a king."

Slaves do not get many compliments. To be praised just causes her to strive that much harder for perfection.

Nellie folded her large arms across the starched white apron covering her big belly and said, "Thank you, Massa, Sir," while looking down at the floor.

Massa Ferguson's favorite meal was fried catfish, collard greens, and baked sweet potatoes, along with hot water, cornbread, and sweet iced tea. Whenever he was home, this meal was served often, and he never got tired of it.

There was no end to what goes on in the late fall at Tall Oaks. The gigantic smokehouse was always filled to capacity by this time of the year, with cured and smoked meats, pork, beef, goat, chicken, turkey, and wild game.

As a general rule, things ran very, very smoothly at Tall Oaks. There was never the stress and worry of being sold if you were a model slave. There was enough money and food to provide security. So often, not enough money was generated to take care of all the slaves on a given plantation. When times got hard because cotton, tobacco, or rice prices go down, slaves had to be sold to cut expenses and to raise cash. In all the years, this had never occurred at Tall Oaks.

Freedom was what every slave craved, not a better slave master or plenty of food to eat while working themselves to death. Complete freedom was the only acceptable solution.

A young but somewhat wise slave replied to the nearest one pulling bolls, "Ain't no freedom in being a slave, would rather be hungry half the time and free."

The old black man next to him said, "Sho nuff you done said a mouthful," and never missed a boll.

The old man looked up to the heaven and began to wail. "Lord, Lord, Lord, look down from the sky. Can you see the tears in our eyes? Reach down from your throne and take us poor slave children home. Bless us with a forever sleep. Deliver us from chopping, picking cotton, and tending sheep. Bless us Lord wif your eternal sleep."

By the time the old man finished his song, the entire field was full of singing and crying. The only way out was death, or so they thought.

Of course, none of the slaves knew where they would go or how they could survive. Many of them just wanted to get back to their beloved homeland, where they could be totally free and happy. Africa was heaven on earth.

The slaves sang, prayed, and cried a lot. Somehow it made them feel better; not content, but better. This was another plea that they sent up to heaven often. "Take me home; take me home since I am no longer allowed to roam. Africa used to be my home, so take me, please, take me up to your throne, hear my plea, hear my cry. Take me to my home in the sky. I need to be free, I need to roam. Take me home, take me home." This particular tune was sung a lot in their church services. Somehow it did lighten their load, for the moment anyway.

Absolutely, no one in the south had ever heard of an ice cave. Dixon and his son, Yancy, discovered a small cave (about the size of the shanty they called home) on the property. They insulated the outside top with leaves and hay, and on the inside, they attached tarps to the roof and sides, even the floor. During the winter, ice was extricated from the lake and stored in the cave. Consequently, fresh meat was available year round, along with ice for cold drinks. During the middle of a hot muggy Tennessee summer, ice cream and iced drinks were a rare treat. Ice was strictly reserved for the big house. Fortunately, food was never a problem. Growing, harvesting and preserving food was a year-round operation.

There was a special rhythm to a busy plantation— chickens clucking and pecking at the ground for food, children playing and working, cows grazing, and field hands silhouetted black against the beautiful blue sky. Every living creature at Tall Oaks was busy, in a world all its own.

Things never changed much at Tall Oaks. The slaves worked harder and harder while the plantation owners got richer and richer. This degradation of human beings must end.

Chapter Two

In the early morning haze, there was not a prettier sight in all of Tennessee than Tall Oaks. The magnificent white mansion set high atop a hill, with a paved brick meandering road leading all the way up the hill, under the portico, and out again. The portico was designed to protect anyone entering or leaving the mansion from the elements. Blooming magnolia trees lined the drive on both sides all the way to the house. The breathtaking white blooms were as big as dinner plates.

Just inside the massive front door was a large gallery entryway. French silk paper adorned the walls, an Italian crystal glass chandelier hangs elegantly from the ceiling, and hand-rubbed wood floors were underfoot. An oval silk rug greets your feet at the door. It was in soft hues of light blue, pink, and beige. A huge round French table set in the entry, just a few feet beyond the rug, and a most impressive, large, lead crystal vase held fresh flowers.

Several feet down the hallway was a drawing room filled with exquisite French furniture, sofas, lounge chairs, and tables; all were beautifully arranged. Ornate gold leaf mirrors on the wall reflect the incredible beauty of the room. The windows were covered with pale blue custom-made draperies that puddle (a true indication of affluence) on the shiny wood floors. On one side of the entry was a large formal dining room as lavish as the other rooms. Off the entry was a winding hand-carved staircase leading to the second floor. Beyond the dining room was a banquet room fit for a king and his queen. The floors were white marble, ideal for dancing. This room also had a white fire-place right in the middle of the outside wall, with doors on each side leading out to a balcony. During the warm summer month's parties, couples dance through one door out to the balcony and in through the other door. Sconces around the walls, loveseats, and high-backed French chairs adorned the room. Back down the hall and through the dining room was the serving kitchen.

Even having a lake on your property was of no help in case of a fire; thus, the reason for a detached kitchen where the cooking was actually done.

Everyone on the plantation was very cautious about fire, including the slaves. Absolutely, no one cooked in their living quarters.

To the very back of the house, on the opposite side of the serving kitchen, was Massa Ferguson's study. Needless to say, it was a large room with the library just down the hall. The room contained pieces of oak furniture, large, overstuffed maroon leather chairs, and couches. On the wooden floor, a large round rug made there on the planta-tion by several of the female slaves. An intricate and painstaking rendition of his prized racehorse was right in the center, surrounded by just the heads of several of his other award-winning stallions. The windows were covered with a fabric that closely resembled burlap—no girlie stuff for his manly room.

On almost any given day, from one to as many as six of Ferguson's business associates and friends stop by and congregate in his den. They smoked cigars, sipped a little brandy, and discussed every subject under the sun. One day, the banker asked, "Why is a male slave allowed up the stairway to your private quarters?"

Ferguson explained, "Dixon is my most trusted and talented slave. He is allowed upstairs to fetch my shoes and boots to shine and repair when needed. I personally chose Annabelle and Dixon to marry. They made a good match. Both were strong, hardworking, and completely trustworthy." Ferguson further explained, "Dixon and Annabelle are inventors, they have made me lots of money." His guests were duly impressed.

The winding staircase led to the bedrooms located on the second floor. The master suite was furnished in fine French furniture, of course. There was a sitting room off the lovely bedroom. The bed had four posters and a pale blue, trimmed-in-white lace canopy. Even in the master bedroom and setting room, the pale blue, pure silk draperies puddled on the floor—a true sign of elegance and wealth. Only two other bedrooms were furnished upstairs. There was no furnished nursery yet. Oriental rugs abound, silk and wool alike, even a long runner extended the entire length of the upstairs hallway. Off the sitting room was a balcony with lots of blooming flowers growing in pots. Miz Lucinda had spent many hours there during the warm months. The view of the lake, the fields, and all the land had been very comforting to her.

After finishing their morning ritual, Annabelle never failed to say, "Miz Lucinda, would you like to enjoy some fresh air?"

She almost never refused, no matter what the weather was like. "That sounds delightful. I love to sit up high and enjoy the view."

Annabelle would attend to the flowers while the lady of the house sat and contemplated what a wonderful life she had.

"Annabelle, you work magic with the flowers. They are truly magnificent."

"Thank you, Ma'am, they is beautiful."

Even in the winter, Miz Annabelle liked sitting on the veranda.

Annabelle would say, "Miz Lucinda, you need to come in, don't want to catch your death of cold, it be cold out here."

The Fergusons love to entertain for business and pleasure. In the spring and fall, elaborate lawn parties were given. Who in their right mind would not enjoy exhibiting this ostentatious dream place, the lush and flawless blue-green lawn, and the tiered brick flowerbeds that extend the entire length of the front of the house? The flowerbeds were ablaze with brilliant colors. On either side of the massive hand-carved front entrance door were invisible wires that held a profusion of blazing red bougainvillea. The roof of the expansive, curved front porch was supported by ten white marble pillars grouped in pairs.

The cook and her many helpers spent a week preparing and taking care of every minute detail. The afternoon of the affair, every table was set with a white Belgian linen tablecloth and napkins, fine china, and sterling silver. Each centerpiece was a crystal bowl with a floating magnolia bloom. It was never the same centerpiece. Sometimes it was an arrangement of flowers grown right on the plantation, all in crystal vases. There were special flowerbeds that provide fresh flowers during the growing season.

Miz Lucinda was very involved in the planning of all the parties. She was in the kitchen, telling the cooks, "You need to use my receipt," for one thing or another, "I will instruct you," "This is the proper way to set the tables" or "Arrange the flowers this way." She would really come alive and display her many talents and great taste.

The ladies were all dressed in cool, lightweight fine-gauge cottons, extra-thin silks, and beautiful prints of the sheerest fabrics. Most of the dresses were imported from France and Italy.

The air was fragrant with the fine imported perfumes. Fiery, beautiful jewels adorned all the ladies.

The waiters, dressed in black pants and white shirts, quickly and quietly serve the honored guests. The group waited with great anticipation.

At the spring and fall lawn parties, the food was always light and delicious. It was not your typical Southern meal. This was mainly due to the ice cave. There was chipped ice for the water, tea, and lemonade. Usually, there would be chilled shrimp cocktail, chilled cucumber soup, cold strawberries, cold chicken, and cold sliced roast beef. Yeast rolls were to die for, along with hand-churned butter.

It went without saying that every summer party was topped off with ice cream. At each occasion, it was different. It could be one of several flavors—strawberry, peach, French vanilla, and chocolate, or maybe butter pecan. It was indeed a treat. No one in Tennessee could boast of serving chilled food, not to mention ice cream in the hot muggy summertime.

Mrs. Ferguson was dressed in a floor length, lightweight, soft pink frock, greeting her guests. "It is so wonderful to see you again, Mary Lou." Mary Lou was wearing a beautiful blue outfit that perfectly matched her eyes, and lots of aquamarine and diamond jewelry. She was thin, gracious, and beautiful, just the opposite of her portly, red-faced, always sweating husband. *They make quite a pair,* thought Lucinda. He was their banker.

Mr. and Mrs. Ferguson greeted their barrister and his wife. Clara and Benson was a lovely couple. He was pale, tall, and thin, with blond hair and expressive brown eyes. Clara was olive, dark-headed, shapely, and beautiful. "Your sheer white ruffled dress is breathtaking," Lucinda said smiling. She was dripping in diamonds and rubies.

"It is wonderful to see you" and "You look great" went on all evening. The Ferguson's minister and his mousey wife were in attendance. She made her dress and was wearing inherited diamond jewelry. The county doctor and his smart and beautiful wife would not miss one of their parties. She was wearing a very lightweight, pale green, designer dress, and emerald jewelry.

The compliments were too numerous to count. "The food is the best I have ever tasted," "Your grounds are the prettiest in the county," "Your servants are spectacular." At each party, the Ferguson's always top themselves.

During the winter months, the parties were taken inside for dinner and dancing. Dinner was served in the elaborate drawing room with the large wood-burning fireplace. After dinner, everyone would dance until dawn in the ballroom. Small comfortable couches and carved French high-backed chairs line the walls, leaving plenty of room for dancing. Ferguson hired musicians from several plantations to provide the music. The music was always excellent! The Ferguson's parties were the talk of the town.

Before the guests depart, coffee would be served in the dining room under the magnificent imported crystal chandeliers, with the pink candles in the wall sconces casting twinkling light down on each and every one of these privileged, arrogant, selfish people.

It was on occasions like the dinner parties or the trips abroad that remind Mr. J.M. Ferguson that he did indeed live a privileged life. It was a genteel Southern life—good food, good wine, lots of money, and slaves at your beck and call. This was heaven on earth.

Mr. Ferguson was a pompous, narcissistic owner of human flesh, who loves to show off and strut and boast. It was an intricate part of his very being.

Extensive travel had helped make J.M. Ferguson head and shoulders above most of his contemporaries. He would travel and learn. The brick paved walkways and drives at Tall Oaks were learned about in New Orleans.

On their honeymoon trip to France, he and Miz Lucinda fell in love with the beautiful, high quality French furniture and accessories. Actually, his bride fell in love with it. Over the years, they filled their home with imported French finery. Very little American-made items were owned by the Fergusons. Perhaps only what was produced on their own plantation. They were indeed the elite of Tennessee.

Whenever Ferguson got a chance, he had to boast, especially when he was in his study with his business associates and friends. This is a good example: "Even slaves can stand out and be favored. Dixon's father was my father's favorite slave. Now, Dixon is my favorite slave. Dixon is quiet, faithful, and very smart, if a slave can be smart. He takes excellent care of the horses, barns, is quite an inventor, and would never consider running away. He has a short leg, making running impossible anyway." Lucky for Massa Ferguson.

When Dixon was very young, just a pup, he was helping his father in one of the barnyards. A horse spooked and stepped on his foot. He limped for several weeks. Massa Ferguson noticed and started talking and paying attention to him. Dixon liked feeling special, thus, the limp. He discovered very quickly that being lame got you noticed and favored by the Massa.

Dixon was also the coachman. He drove the Ferguson's everywhere. Absolutely, no one but Dixon ever drove the Brougham two-passenger, drop-top carriage or the elaborate four-passenger town coach with its solid wood panels and glass windows. Either of these vehicles could only be owned by the well-to-do like the Fergusons.

Of course, Dixon dressed the part of the "coachman to the rich." He wore a top hat, riding boots, white shirt, and tapered black pants that fit inside the boots. His outfit and wonderful Southern manners made the Fergusons very proud. Everyone in town knew Dixon by what he drove and how awesome he looked.

Dixon would assist the Ferguson's into their coach or carriage. He would then smile, and click his heels. He played the part of a slave to the hilt.

All the while, he was daydreaming about the day a darkie in a monkey suit will drive him and his missus around in a fancy carriage. The day would come. Of this he was sure.

He wondered, "Why can't I just be Dixon, not Dixon Boy or just boy." To never be called a boy again was going to be music to his ears.

Miz Lucinda depended on Annabelle for everything, from coiffing her hair to helping her dress, and even in supplying her birth control, but more about that later. Annabelle kept the master bedroom in perfect order with rose scented sheets from her own homemade scented elixir and fresh flowers every day. She also kept the downstairs perfect at all times. The imported French furniture was treasured and expensive. Only Annabelle knew how to take proper care of it. Miz Ferguson had been collecting expensive cut glass, such as Stuben, Baccarat, and Waterford. Only Annabelle was allowed to touch the misses prized pieces.

Dixon and Annabelle were both strong in their own ways. Ferguson saw this clearly. He allowed them to court briefly and get married. They would produce strong, obedient, and somewhat smart offsprings. And so they did. Their children were not lame, only Dixon. He rocked himself, and appeared to swing and rock just to walk. It certainly did not seem to slow him down.

On a 2,000-acre plantation, the work was never finished. The days began at the crack of dawn. The "overseer" rode through the slave quarters and banged on a drum to wake everybody up. They would hurriedly dress—children and all—and rush down to one of the two slave kitchens on either end of their row of shanties. Other slaves who had prepared an ample breakfast, would remain behind and clean the kitchens and the slave quarters. This was done on a rotating basis. Massa Ferguson truly believed that cleanliness was essential. It kept down germs, and thus, illnesses.

If there was any new assignment, the "overseer," or Massa Ferguson, would bring it to the slaves' attention. Otherwise, one day was exactly like the one before.

Massa Ferguson frequently traveled to Europe, New Orleans, and all over. So often, Bo, the "overseer," the next in command, would give the orders.

When Massa Ferguson was home, he rode over every inch of his land, watching, checking to see if everyone was maintaining his code of excellence. All the barns, fields, gardens, washhouses, everything was inspected by Massa Ferguson himself. He kept his finger on the pulse of things.

Massa Ferguson knew the names of all the slaves and their responsibilities. He would walk around, saying in his loud voice, "How are the baby chicks doing?"

"Good, Massa. All hatched none died."

"Very good, Moses, keep up the good work. Good morning, Helen, Mary, and Liza, how is the canning coming along?"

"Two mo weeks, Massa, everything is gwine be done."

"Very good, nobody will have to go hungry," he would say with a smile.

However long it takes, the Massa never stopped until the tedious job was completed. On rare occasions, it would take a week or longer. Nothing escaped his watchful eyes.

The slaves got off at 3:00 P.M. on Saturdays and did not go back to work until Monday at daybreak, with the exception of the household help. They got half days off during the week.

There were crops to be planted, chopped, or harvested. Then the fields had to be prepared to start all over again. The small children brought water, picked up rocks and stumps, or whatever was required of them. Everybody worked!

Six days a week, there was laundry to wash, dry, and iron, and always, work clothes to be mended. The delicate finery from the big house was done on separate days with milder soap. Some of the slaves do nothing but wash and mend from the age of about ten until death.

If his unpaid help were well fed, healthy, and clean, their production was so much greater. Everything at Tall Oaks was perfection up to, and including, the slaves. The ones not born on the plantation were all handpicked by the Massa himself.

Chapter Three

A stand of tall oak trees dichotomized the extremity of the haves and the have-nots, the free and the slave, the educated and the uneducated, the blacks and the whites. These two worlds were less than a quarter of a mile apart, separated by nothing more than oak trees reaching for the heavens. These two worlds were light-years apart in reality.

Massa Ferguson's grandfather settled this 2,000 acres. There were only two major things on the land at that time—the very noticeable stand of tall pin oak trees in a long row and the peaceful and beautiful lake, thus, the name Tall Oaks. Over many years, great improvements had been made and great heartaches had been wrought.

All the rustic wooden slave shanties were exactly alike—one long room with beds, and a fireplace to keep warmed by in the cold months. There were no windows, just a front and back door and wooden floors. The meager accommodations were provided by the plantation owner on his property. Learning to read was against the law. Only Annabelle could practice medicine. J.M. Ferguson made up his own rules because she saved him money; no doctors were needed. A poor slave was a stranger in a strange land. In this land, you are be trapped like a helpless dumb animal. Blacks had no rights here. You are on the same level as the farm animals, except that you walk on two legs instead of four.

In the still of the night, in one of the shanties, you could hear a male voice saying: "You is the lub of my life. I done promised to take care of you and I's gwine find a way to find out about de underground railroad. We is gwine git free, go North."

A softer voice…"I is gwine keep on wid my herbs, potions, elixirs, and cures. Dat just may come in right handy purdy soon," said his mate. They would no longer be at the beck and call of their white owners.

Behind each shanty, the slaves were allowed to grow their favorite fruit and vegetables in their own gardens. Saturday evening and all day Sunday, they were free to cook in either of the two large, fully equipped slave kitchens.

One family, in particular, had a large herb garden. The wife tended her herbs, dried them, and made potions, and everything imaginable from her herbs. Annabelle was a master at her craft.

Twice a year, the plantation workers would line up for their spring and fall tonic. It was rare that anyone needs any other medicine. Of course, Annabelle had special potions for the pregnant women, and later their babies. She kept everybody strong and healthy.

A long area behind the shanty and the herb garden had been cleared away. This area was for running sprints, doing squats, and endurance and strength building. The time would come when they would need to be strong and fleet of foot. Dixon and his family exercised every evening.

Once in a while, another slave would come to the plantation needing to barter and to have something repaired. There were slaves at Tall Oaks who could do anything. Sometimes Dixon was able to get to talk and find out what was going on outside of his small world from one of these slaves in need of repair work. Dixon would do the work while talking, but mostly listening for any information he was unaware of. Bridles, saddles, and many other pieces of farm equipment kept both of them busy all day long. Later that evening, the slave left with a wagon full of repaired farm essentials for which Massa Ferguson was paid, paid for Dixon's labor and knowledge.

The obsession with being healthy and fit had to do with what Dixon and Annabelle had heard about—the "underground railroad." As much as they could understand, it was a complicated system of escape routes leading from the South into the North, Midwest, and even Canada. Some slaves were so disgusted with the United States, especially the south, that they escaped all the way to Haiti and the Bahamas. There were no white Massas there. It was more like the place that their forefathers had left behind. With the "underground railroad," secret names and codes were used: the "stations" were places of shelter; the "agents" were those men and women who help the runaways; and the "conductors" were supervisors who handle travel arrangements.

It was rumored that an ex-slave runaway, named Harriet Tubman, helped free more than 300 slaves. She was small, tough, and clever. She spoke in a raspy voice. In the event that she led you to freedom, was quite an experience. You had to be physically fit and ready to run long and hard. If you got snakebitten, you could not scream. You had to keep moving, praying all the time that the varmint was not poisonous. The faint of heart could never make a run for freedom. It was a run that only the very strong could successfully make. Unfortunately, bloodhounds would be on your heels and snakes would be in your path. Should a bite turn out to be poisonous, the victim simply dropped in their tracks, and the others stepped over the dying body. They must continue their flight to freedom. Time was of the essence.

Despite help, it was still a very dangerous mission, hiding in the woods and abandoned houses by day, and by night riding in wagons, underneath hay and what have you. It was an audacious journey. If you could make it to Buffalo, New York on a steamboat, you would be a free person. Slavery does not exist in the North.

William Wells Brown, a crew member, helped slip non-paid, fugitive black slaves to safety. New York was a free state, but Canada was certainly more acceptable and accommodating to the blacks. A quote from William Wells Brown: "And while on the lake, I always make arrangements to carry the runaways on the boat to Buffalo or Detroit and thus affect their escape to the "Promised Land.""

In 1842, between the first of May and the first of December, Brown ferried sixty-nine fugitives across the lake, assisting them on the last leg of their journey to freedom. Some of them had been on the road for many weeks. In some cases, months had passed since they had last been under a slave owner's command, subject to every whim, and prisoner to the whip.

Northerners wanted to prevent the spread of slavery into new states or to abolish it altogether. But Southerners, with an agricultural economy, heavily depended on slave labor, and were in no position to give up their source. Free workers were their lifeline.

Dixon and Annabelle knew that they might get the opportunity to flee to freedom, so they had to be ready. In the privacy of their shanty, they talked and thought about the "underground railroad." They made plans. There was one thing for sure and certain, if their escape was not successful, they would be torn apart as a family forever. Massa Ferguson would sell them off, one by one. They both knew full well he would. To be separated from his family, Dixon thought, would be a fate worse than death. There had to be another way, a better way.

During Dixon and Annabelle's time in their shanty, they always talked to each other like they were already free. "Dixon, honey, when you go to town this morning, please buy some coffee, and do not forget to go to the post office." Annabelle would kiss his cheek, smile, and say, "Thank you, my love."

The children, Yancy and Dixiebelle, would talk with a breathless Southern accent in almost perfect English. The boy talked in a booming voice like the Massa. Sometimes he would say, "This work is becoming intolerable, I need to go away for a while." He would look at his sister and say, "Bo, handle things until my return." This kind of role playing went on for several years. The entire process helped them "keep hope alive."

For the time being, Dixon and Annabelle had to continue to be contrite, cooperative, and ever watchful. Their time for freedom was soon to come.

On this 2,000-acre plantation there had been three generations of slaves. Dixon declared to his God in heaven…"Slavery will end with this generation." Every day he sent this declaration to the heavens.

He and his beloved Annabelle knew full well that no man has the right to own another human being. Massa Ferguson was paid for their labor, their inventions, and their loyalty. Take these things away and the Massa wasn't even as smart as half of the oppressed black people he kept under his thumb. These two were sure of that.

Chapter Four

Massa Ferguson kept a half dozen bloodhounds in a dog run not far from one of the barns. From time to time, there would be as few as two dogs enclosed. Other slave owners would borrow the dogs to track down their own runaway slaves. Ferguson insisted that his dogs were the very best in the county. Every plantation owner in the area was welcome to use the dogs. It was good public relations.

At the town meetings and church services, Ferguson never failed to announce, "My bloodhounds are the best trackers around. Anyone needing to catch their runaway slaves feel free to borrow mine. Keep them watered and let them run."

What no one knew, at that time, was that the slaves who got away rubbed red onion or spruce pine on the soles of their shoes, then over their entire bodies. Those two aromas permeated the woods. No human scent existed. When this particular event occurred, the dogs would run in circles, crisscross a wide area, and, finally, return to their origin of departure exhausted, confused, and barking wildly. Even the dogs knew that the runaways were out there, but they just could not pick up their scent. Sometimes they would come within a few feet of a runaway, but to no avail.

The runaways that were caught and returned to their owners were beaten within an inch of their lives. The beatings really didn't deter any of them. They were motivated by so many negative factors. New mothers were relieved of their duties for only two weeks, field hands and all. Many of them dropped in their tracks. They simply were not given enough time to recover from childbirth. Oftentimes, a husband or wife was chosen by the Massa. This was viewed by the slaves as inhuman. Even a short courtship period would have been helpful and greatly appreciated.

One woman, a field hand, took her infant son to the cotton field two weeks after birth. She could only nurse him twice in the course of a work day. Her breasts were painfully engorged with milk. The boy was hungry most of the day.

Hanna, the child's mother, chopped cotton at a steady pace, head bowed, tears streaming from her eyes, and blood trickling down her legs. She never took her eyes off Bo, the "overseer." He sat tall in the saddle to observe every single thing going on in the fields. Just as the "overseer" galloped out of sight, Hanna sneaked back to check on her infant boy. Hanna started running in the direction Bo rode off. Running and screaming "Missa Bo, Missa Bo" arms flailing in the air. Bo reined in his horse and quickly headed back in the direction of the screaming, agitated female slave.

"Come, Missa Bo, de snake done kilt my boy!" All the commotion was over a big black snake that had wrapped itself around the baby up to his chin. Only about six or eight inches of the snake's body was still on the ground. Maybe the part left on the ground was for leverage. You could see the muscles slowly easing the creature closer to the baby's mouth and nose.

In an instant, the overseer sized up the situation dismounted and with one swift movement, he grabbed the snake by the tail, which sent the child spinning like a top. Bo slammed the snake's head on the hard, hot, crusty ground, killing it in an instant. By this time, the baby was awakened, hungry and crying. Another minute would have been too late. The snake was slowly covering the infant's mouth and nose in an attempt to smother its prey.

Mr. Bo told Hanna, "Feed and quiet your child down, then return to work." How many other babies who were left unattended in the fields on plantations had met a tragic death such as this almost was? The snake would have smothered the child and discovered that he was too large to swallow. Consequently, he would just quietly slide back into the undergrowth, never to be seen again. The baby's death would have been a complete mystery forever.

Hanna put her baby in a safer place and returned to work. In a sad, barely audible voice, she began to sing: "In my home in the sky, ain't gwine cry, cry, no mo, no mo, nooo mo, nooo mo. In my home in the sky, ain't gwine hoe, hoe no mo, no mo, no mo nooo mo. In my home in the sky, we all gwine sing, sing and dance, sing and dance, sing and dance, and never grow tired, tired, no mo, no mo, nooo mo. In my home in the sky, we will have wings, wings, and fly, fly, fly, and be free, free as the clouds in the sky. Forever mo, forever mo, forever mooo!"

About halfway through the song, all the field hands joined in. At this moment, death was the only way out. Hanna sent up yet another prayer to heaven for the freedom of her baby boy and her entire family. Heaven was bombarded every day with such prayers. These were prayers and pleas from every living slave. Prayers are always answered, it might just take a while, but they are always answered. The field hands continued to chop, cry, moan, and sing.

A few minutes before Bo blew the whistle near sundown to quit working and head home, yet another incident occurred. The oldest female in the field suddenly crumpled to the ground like yesterday's laundry. Bo turned her over. Her breathing was shallow and her heartbeat faint. All these were due to age, too many years of hard work, heat stroke, influenza, and lack of rest. She had been bone tired for years.

Of course, Annabelle, the plantation slave doctor, would pay a visit once the old sick woman is taken to her shanty. Upon her arrival to look after the old woman, Annabelle immediately noticed how thin, wrinkled, and exhausted she looked. She then set about making the poor old soul as comfortable as possible. Her vital signs were checked. In a few minutes, Annabelle walked outside and told the "overseer," "Direct the coffin making. It will be needed no later than a day and a half, maybe even sooner. The old field hand is dying."

Two days later, the slave's death was entered in the master record book that was kept in Massa Ferguson's study in his big oak desk. The funeral lasted less than thirty minutes. There was very little her children or anyone could say. She was just a slave. She was buried in the cemetery right there on the plantation. Everyone returned to their appointed duties. Just another day at Tall Oaks.

In retrospect, what can you say about a field hand slave? She was dedicated, but she had no choice! She was a hard worker. What choice did she have? There was not one thing anyone could say that would differentiate that old dead slave from any of the others. She had been born, worked, cried, prayed, and then died. Not much of a life, just the life of a slave.

Several weeks later, Bo donned his handsome new black snakeskin boots, made by the cobblers on the plantation. They were a constant reminder to Hanna of that awful day, a day she would like to forget.

From time to time, all the slaves at Tall Oaks were gathered to witness the brutal beatings of runaway slaves from other plantations. This exhibition was staged to remind them to never even try running, and also to demonstrate to them how lucky they were to belong to Massa Ferguson. He did not believe in beatings, but there were worse things in life than beatings. Being worked to death was one, dehumanized and treated worse than the farm animal was another. Things never changed for a slave. They worked harder and harder while their owners got richer and richer, all on their tired backs.

Once, many years ago, a certain slave named Amos worked in the hemp field at harvest time. Massa Ferguson admonished all the workers not to smoke or experiment with his cash crop. Rope and work clothes were made from hemp for use on the plantation. Hemp would also make you high if you smoke the dried leaves like a hand rolled cigarette.

All month long, Amos worked hard and mumbled to himself. "Do not want no Massa telling me what to do? Tired of being a slave, I will steal some hemp and smoke it anytime I please." He really worked himself into a lather.

Amos was born at Tall Oaks, but always had great difficulty accepting being a slave. He had muttered to himself since he could talk, "I is tall, thin, and fleet of foot, kin run like a gazelle. Someday I ain't gwine be no slave!"

His wife pleaded with tears in her eyes, "Please, Amos, think of your family. If you get caught, you will be sold."

"Wife, I get free and come back and get you and the children, I give you my word."

After work that day, ole Amos took his stash out and smoked all evening. The longer he smoked, the braver he became. Shortly after dark, he decided to make a run for his freedom. He ran like the wind for a few miles, sat down, and smoked again. He stumbled around in the woods, cursed, cried, and prayed. He really wanted his freedom, but he did not think it through very well. Needless to say, by daybreak, the hounds caught up to him.

Amos was never whipped. Over a period of two years, each of his five children and his wife were sold off one by one. And last but not least, Amos was sold to one of the meanest plantation owners to ever own a slave. The hurt from this kind of treatment lasted longer and hurts deeper than being whipped ever could. This poor slave never saw any of his family again. A few years later, it was reported that he died, beaten to death by his new owner.

On almost any given day, one to three of Ferguson's friends would visit Tall Oaks—his barrister, the banker, and one of several plantation owner bigwigs. Everything under the sun was discussed in the privacy of that study.

Once the barrister said, "What is that slave doing, going up your stairs?"

Ferguson replied, "His father before him did the very same thing. He takes my shoes and boots and 'spit shines' every pair. He is my best and most trusted slave. Dixon, he is called. The boy drives me everywhere, helps me shop, goes all over town without me, and has never even thought about running away. As you can see, he is lame. Legs don't work quite right. One leg is shorter than the other, so I allowed him and Annabelle, my wife's personal maid, to briefly court and marry. It has been a good union. She saves me lots of money and makes me lots of money. She is the plantation doctor, better than any medical school doctor I ever met. She can treat and cure anything. Annabelle delivers all the babies here at Tall Oaks and treats all the farm animals. There is nobody better! Practicing medicine is illegal for a slave, but at Tall Oaks, I am the law!" His friends laughed and agreed with him.

The Massa continued, "Her husband, Dixon, has invented several things worthy of a patent, to which I hold, have had manufactured, and make money on. He also devised an ice cave. Your drinks are cold and refreshing, thanks to Dixon, his ice cave, and the invention of his ice crusher."

Massa Ferguson enjoyed having his friends visit him very much. He loved to boast and show off. To the banker he would say, "Any plans to add on or build a larger bank, just to hold my money? It is coming in almost faster than I can keep track of it." Ferguson strutted when he walked and boasted when he talked.

All manner of subjects were discussed in the rustic comfortable study! The fact was that slaves were lower than the farm animals and have no human feelings whatsoever. The only major difference was that the slaves walk on two legs, farm animals walk on four. All plantation owners agree that slaves were born to work and serve for free!

Earlier that day, Miz Lucinda, the mistress of Tall Oaks, was stretching and waking up. She could hear the faint swishing of Annabelle's starched and ironed dress with the stiff white apron over it.

Before even ascending the stairs, Annabelle went through the serving kitchen and into the small ante room and washed her face and hands thoroughly. Prior to serving Miz Lucinda's breakfast, she had already cleaned the entire downstairs except the kitchen. The cooks took care of the kitchen and the room behind it.

While she slowly enjoyed her food, her bed was made with fresh rose scented sheets. The mistress of the house went behind a silk screen and washed in warm water with the perfumed soap assembled on the console, and then dressed herself in the attire that Annabelle had selected and laid out for her.

While Miz Lucinda was attending to this chore, the chamber pot was quickly and discreetly removed to the hall to be picked up and emptied by one of the other maids. Annabelle moved about the magnificent room, cleaning and straightening.

Upon emerging from behind the screen, Miz Lucinda sat at her dressing table. The daily ritual began. First, her beautiful golden tresses were brushed, then curled, and arranged to perfection by Annabelle. Next, her face was made up. Some of the cosmetics were made by Annabelle herself. Miz Lucinda was partial to her many shades of lipstick and her under makeup moisturizers.

Miz Lucinda turned to her personal maid, smiled, and said, "Whatever would I do without you, Annabelle, my favorite person in the whole world? Did you finish the downstairs?"

"Yes, Miz Lucinda," replied Annabelle.

"Very good. Let's go to town and shop. Tell Dixon we will be ready in one hour and have the carriage under the portico."

Miz Lucinda told Annabelle, "Put on one of my best silk dresses and wear the ivory combs I gave you in your long beautiful silky hair and my favorite cameo on your dress."

Before today, Miz Lucinda had never offered one of her dresses, especially a silk one. The fabric felt so wonderful on her skin. If she were free and able to earn money, she would wear a silk dress every Sunday to church, she thought to herself.

Annabelle was never comfortable wearing Miz Lucinda's jewelry, but she did. The large, four-poster bed held more than just the large feather bed that Miz Lucinda slept on. All four posters were secret compartments to hide Miz Lucinda's most valuable jewels, gold coins, and other valuables. "A lady has to have even more security than her husband can afford, rich or not."

This secret was strictly between Miz Lucinda and Annabelle. These two women had lots of secrets.

The two women were a sight for sore eyes, a tall, statuesque, green-eyed, blond and a tall, well-figured mulatto, laughing, talking, and having a grand time. Dixon followed behind them, carrying the packages.

Miz Ferguson refused to go into the quaint little tearoom on Main Street because Annabelle was not allowed to accompany her. "We will have tea back at Tall Oaks later," Miz Lucinda assured Annabelle.

From all outward appearances, Miz Ferguson thought of and treated Annabelle as an equal, a confidant and best friend. There were so many secrets shared between these two. In fact, Annabelle kept the two of them supplied with a certain elixir that prevents pregnancy, a secret brought from Africa. The female slaves were to have strong, healthy babies to keep slavery going full steam in the South. A pampered Southern wife was to have children to carry on the name and legacy and produce heirs for the rich plantation owner. At this particular time, neither woman cared in the least about having babies, each one having their own reasons.

Chapter Five

Massa J.M. Ferguson prided himself on being able to hand-pick a smart slave. That unique ability really paid off. Back from a lengthy European trip, Massa took a whole week to check on every square foot of his property and each and every slave. He was in for a profitable surprise. Upon entering one of the barns, he observed Dixon putting clods of dirt into a contraption attached to the edge of the table. He was cranking out pea size pieces of dirt.

"Dixon, what are you doing?" questioned the Massa.

"Howdy do, Sir, welcome home. I done come up with something nice and good for you and the misses, chipped ice from this here thing," replied Dixon. "The ice cave gives you ice in the summertime. This will give you chipped ice for your lemonade, tea and other drinks, all the time, anytime."

Massa Ferguson said, "Well, thank you, Dixon. Whatever would I do without you?" He took the interesting gadget and left.

As Ferguson walked leisurely back up the hill to the big house, he was already making plans to patent and have the ice crusher manufactured, thus, making lots of money. The people back East would all want to own one. His slaves were his greatest assets. They made him money "hands over fist."

Annabelle and Miz Lucinda had spent a lot of time together. They understood each other as much as was humanly possible. They were much like sisters. The only difference between them was that one was a humble slave and servant and the other is a rich, pampered, and free person—the proud owner of human beings. The difference was as different as heaven is to hell.

Massa Ferguson went into his study, sat at his massive desk, and thought about the many inventions devised right on his own plantation. His life was rich and full indeed.

Dixon and Annabelle discovered a formula to feed the beautiful horses raised right on Ferguson's land. The horses' coats were thick and shiny, their bones were extra strong, and their lung capacity was almost double. The race horses were superior to all the others in Tennessee.

Ferguson contemplated the ice cave. What manner of person could come up with something that revolutionary, having no education, no exposure, nothing? No one but Dixon. Ferguson decided that the heavens were pouring out the blessings just for him.

It never occurred to Ferguson that these people had a mind, a soul, and a purpose. Did he not have a conscience? In his mind, these possessions, his property, were purchased by him to be used, exploited, and owned lock, stock, and barrel. They were no different than farm animals, beasts of burden. Slaves were not even listed in the census. They were only listed as property or assets. Slaves were not considered human.

Life could not be better for the Fergusons, owners of Tall Oaks Plantation. There were plenty of slaves to keep them wealthy, keep everything orderly and beautiful, and to wait on them hand and foot. Good food, good times, a good life. There is nothing in the world better than gracious, genteel Southern living.

Annabelle cleaned the downstairs until it sparkled, and then quickly ascended the ornate hand-carved winding staircase with a breakfast tray in hand. It was time to attend to Miz Lucinda's needs. Their daily ritual would begin. Annabelle entered the room, but instead of finding her still lounging in bed, Miz Lucinda was sitting in a fancy blue silk French chair by the window, viewing her face in a silver hand mirror. She appeared distressed. Her first comment was not, "Good morning, lovely day, nice to see you, Annabelle." None of the usual trivia. The first words out of her mouth were, "Annabelle, do you think I am pretty?"

Annabelle replied, "Yes, Miz Lucinda, you is the prettiest lady in all of Tennessee, everybody done knows that."

Miz Lucinda's face broke into a big smile. In her sweetest Southern voice she said, "Thank you, Annabelle. My life at Tall Oaks would be unbearable if it were not for you and your kind ways. Mr. Ferguson is away so much. What on earth could possibly keep him away or intrigue him more than his own wife and his wonderful life here at Tall Oaks? These kinds of thoughts make me uneasy."

Annabelle just shook her bowed head and thought, *Just maybe being free to go and come as you please is not the greatest thing in the world, and others can get hurt as a result of so much freedom.*

Miz Lucinda continued to express her concerns about her life and her husband. Annabelle continued to make her bedroom perfect. She left the room briefly and brought back a vase of fresh flowers. They made the missus smile.

Annabelle was so much smarter and more perceptive than Miz Lucinda could ever imagine. People may be forced to stay where they are not happy, but no one stays away from where they are happy. A poor slave woman certainly did not know much, but of this she was sure.

"Now, Miz Lucinda, do not fret none. You and the Massa are a perfect couple. He loves you very much. He is just a busy businessman…one of the richest in the country." Still looking down Annabelle shook her head up and down to confirm her convictions.

This particular day turned out to be like no other one before it. The life of a poor, uneducated slave changed on a whim. As Annabelle coiffed Miz Lucinda's hair, quite out of the clear blue sky, Miz Lucinda said, "I don't really like to do needle work, play cards, or talk to any of these old biddies that come to call. I need a hobby, a true calling. My calling involves you Annabelle. I went to college to be a teacher. You are going to be my pupil. I will teach you to read, do math, and learn until you are a real scholar. It will be our secret." Miz Lucinda smiled and said, "When we finish, you will read and speak like an educated lady."

Annabelle thought to herself, *Something is going on. Massa Ferguson not doing right, gone from home too much, and Miz Lucinda knows or suspects something.* She keeps her head down but thinking all the time. *Ain't nothing as it should be in this white folks' world.* She was thinking so hard, she was shaking her head from side to side, quite unaware of her action.

In all the years, Annabelle had been the personal maid and companion to Miz Lucinda. She had never seen her so happy. Her green eyes sparkled. She smiled and even waltzed around the room. She giggled like a school girl. "Annabelle, I just adore having secrets. It truly, will be our secret! It makes me happy."

Annabelle's heart was beating so fast she could hardly breathe. She and Dixon had tried in vain to teach themselves to read. First of all, it was against the law, Secondly, it was not easy. Neither of them even knew where to start, but they tried, to no avail.

Deep down in her soul, Annabelle knew this was the beginning of something incredible! The ability to read and write would open up a whole new world for her and her family. Slaves or not, their lives were about to change. She could feel it in her soul…

A few weeks later, Massa Ferguson left on one of his infamous trips to New Orleans. The very next day, time was set aside. The teaching and the learning began. Both women were two happy fulfilled people. Behind locked doors in Massa Ferguson's study, six days a week, for at least an hour and a half, or sometimes longer, the mistress of Tall Oaks was teaching; the humble slave was learning.

Miz Lucinda smiled, preened, and taught. "Annabelle, we will start at the very beginning, the alphabet. Repeat after me and try to pronounce exactly as I do."

Annabelle tried very hard. It was not easy, but she did learn. After a few short months, she could even read very simple children's books. She was making progress.

Every day before class, Annabelle would say, "Thank you so much, Miz Lucinda. I can actually read like a smart white person."

"Annabelle, you cannot imagine how happy that makes me."

Chapter Six

As close as these two women were, there were still secrets between them. Miz Lucinda did not know her husband nearly as well as she should have.

Massa Ferguson spent an inordinate amount of time away from home, in Europe and all over the south, especially in New Orleans. His lovely, cultured, and well versed wife had only been to Europe once since she married. The last year of college, she was given a trip to Paris, France as part of her graduation gift. Growing up, she and her rich family went to Europe every year. Miz Lucinda absolutely did not get to tour the south with her husband. He always said, "It is too trying, too hard to travel with slaves to care for you." Or, "It is just boring business." The two of them did vacation back East in the fall every year. Mr. Ferguson had a brother whose family lived in New York City. Her husband always treated her like a beautiful china doll. Life was not all bad.

While Annabelle was grooming Miz Lucinda one morning, she started to talk. "I never dreamed my life would end up like this, trapped in a loveless marriage, married to a stranger. What can a thirty-year-old divorced woman do—go home to her parents or go east to New York and teach school? My greatest revenge is to stay right here at his precious Tall Oaks and teach you to read and write under his very nose."

Annabelle was overcome with so many emotions that she could not begin to understand. Her tears flowed freely as she hung her bowed head even lower. Her brain was saying, dance, sing, and laugh. But in all honesty, her heart was breaking at this moment for her oppressor. It seemed nobody's life is perfect.

Mr. Jesse Monroe Ferguson had a secret life that only he and his second family in New Orleans knew about.

About six years ago, Jesse Ferguson had business with a prominent banker in New Orleans. His life was about to change forever. Across the street from the bank appeared a Southern lady and her personal maid. They certainly were not paying any mind to Mr. Ferguson. But he stopped dead in his tracks and stared. The mulatto slave was the most magnificent creature he had ever seen, beautiful and graceful. He was totally mesmerized. The two of them turned the corner and were soon out of his line of vision. Ferguson's heart was pounding and his palms were clammy. *What just happened?* he thought to himself.

The bank business went smoothly. The funds had been delivered a few days before his arrival. Everything was in order, only needing his approval and signature. As he started to leave the bank, J.M. casually asked the banker, "Who is the lady with the mulatto maid shopping on Front Street? What plantation does her husband own?"

Ferguson returned to his hotel, had lunch, and tried to take a nap. His mind was racing, he felt feverish. What in tarnation was wrong with him? Until today, emotions had never been a part of his makeup. Heretofore, he had prided himself on being a real man's man. Always thinking and making decisions with a clear, unemotional head. Everything with J.M. was business. He raced downstairs to the lobby of the hotel and arranged to hire a carriage to transport him to Whispering Springs Plantation, owned by a Mr. Cornelius Muse, according to his banker.

During the half-hour carriage ride, J.M. thought about what he was going to say. He felt stupid! No, more like a tongue-tied schoolboy. Mr. Ferguson was in control at all times, fair but hard. Was he crazy? Why on God's green earth was he pining after some mulatto he had only gotten a glance of from afar? Why was he so happy inside? Maybe he was losing his mind.

On that too brief carriage ride to the Whispering Springs Plantation, it became crystal clear that all these many years, he had not been happy. He was empty inside, cold, broken, and so lonely he could die. J.M. was simply on a mission seeking happiness. Only God knew how it would end. Mr. J.M. Ferguson, for the first time in his life, was not in control. He had dropped the reins and let his guard down.

A white uniformed female slave let him in and asked his name, then proceeded to fetch Massa Muse. Mr. Muse greeted Ferguson warmly and suggested they sit on the south porch. There was a cool breeze outside, not so inside. At first, the two men introduced themselves and made small talk and sized each other up.

Mr. Ferguson cleared his throat and began, "Sir, is the mulatto, your wife's personal maid, for sale? You name the price!"

"Do you own a plantation, Sir?" inquired Mr. Muse.

"Yes, Sir, but this may sound strange to you. I would like to buy the young woman and court her right here in your parlor and squire her around your beautiful grounds.

If the courtship does not work out, you will have your money and still retain your slave. Sir, I am a man of my word."

Mr. Muse gave him a quizzical stare and said, "Mr. Ferguson, my wife is going to hate to lose Sadie Beth, but you drive a hard bargain. You just offered me a deal I cannot refuse."

"Now, Mr. Muse, I can depend on you to keep the 'bucks' away from Miss Sadie Beth, can I not?"

"That will be no problem, Sir," replied Mr. Muse.

Mr. Ferguson walked to the waiting carriage, entered, and rode away without a backward glance. The deal was sealed, and so was his fate.

Upon Massa Ferguson's return to Tall Oaks, he whistled, he hummed, and he appeared to be happier than he had been in years. He was most attentive and kind to his beautiful wife, Lucinda. All the while implementing his secret plans.

Every spring and fall since they had been married, the Ferguson's gave elaborate seasonal lawn parties. This year was no exception. The outdoor parties were always held on the expansive front lawn. Tables were set with white linen tablecloths and napkins, fine china, crystal, and sterling silver.

There was nothing in this world that the Ferguson's like better than showing off their exquisite surroundings and their antebellum mansion. The waiters in white starched coats and black trousers quietly and quickly serve course after course of fine cuisine, fit for royalty, much to everyone's delight.

Thanks to the ice cave and the ice crusher, cold soups in bowls embedded in chipped ice were served—cool soups like chilled cucumber along with chilled strawberry and chilled cantaloupe. Everything in spring and fall was either chilled or cold. There was cold roast beef, cold fried chicken, chilled green salad, iced water, iced mint tea, and last but not least, ice cream. What an absolute treat. Charming Mrs. Ferguson and gracious Mr. Ferguson were the toast of Tennessee. There was no couple more envied than them.

The "Winter Ball" was the biggest social event of the year, held in late January. Of course, the Ferguson's were the host and hostess of the spectacular event every year. People travelled from far and wide to attend. Each couple hoped and prayed that it does not snow or become icy. This was a social occasion not to be missed.

To begin with, the expansive front lawn was sprayed green for effect. The extraordinary white mansion looked divine on the green setting. Every tree, bush, and plant was trimmed and shaped to its beautiful best. There was nothing left to chance to compromise the look of utter perfection.

Everyone goes into the elegant drawing room first. Champagne was served in crystal flutes on ornate sterling trays, and the party began. The gigantic, blazing white marble fireplace set the cozy tone for a perfect evening. The crystal sconces along the wall and the chandeliers were illuminated by hundreds of pale pink candles. Pink was very flattering to everyone and everything. The entire room sparkled and shined like diamonds. The large silk Oriental rug underfoot was breathtaking.

The ladies had on their finest, from incredibly beautiful ball gowns to millions of dollars in precious jewels. The room was fragrant with the scent of their expensive French perfumes. Mrs. Ferguson was wearing an emerald green silk taffeta gown to match her green eyes. With diamond and emerald jewelry, she was the belle of the ball.

As the evening progressed, everyone moved into the dining room to feast on the most extravagant formally served meal. Champagne glasses were kept filled. The food was served with pure precision. What a proud moment for the Ferguson's. The raves and compliments just kept coming from their rich, sophisticated, and well traveled guests. Mrs. Ferguson was most proud that they both had traveled so extensively. They never failed to bring back a wealth of knowledge and class about gracious living and many other things. When they travel together, it was strictly for pleasure and exposure to the finer things in life.

Finally, the guests went into the grand ballroom, with a smaller white fireplace and a white marble floor, just wonderful for dancing. In this room were sconces along the walls. Much to everyone's delight, right in the center of the room was an elevated area with a full band. The band members were slaves from all over Tennessee. They represent the best of the best on their particular instrument.

Everyone danced into the wee hours of the morning. A good time was had by all!

Chapter Seven

Life was good for Massa Ferguson of Tall Oaks, but apparently not good enough. With all the money made from the slaves, the wonderful parties, good friends, and his sweet, lovely, educated wife, J.M. was still very lonely.

His plight came to an end once he started courting Sadie Beth from the Muse Plantation in New Orleans. He found her to be pure and simple. She listened to him and wanted so much to learn from him. He shared his vast knowledge and wonderful wisdom with her.

J.M. Ferguson was a changed man. He became easier to get along with, he smiled more, even laughed out loud. It was just amazing and he did not question the change.

For many months, J. M. and Sadie Beth courted. She asked almost immediately, "Will you help me talk pretty? I love how you talk." He held her hand, smiled, and said, "I plan to teach you more good things than you can ever imagine."

After six months of courting Sadie Beth, he knew for sure that he had met his soul mate. She was a complete opposite of Miz Lucinda. She was small, almost childlike, sweet to the core, willing to please, and grateful to a fault.

The fact that she was a mulatto did not enter into their lives. They were just two people who were very much in love. J. M. bought a lovely house, furnished it beautifully, and took his love to her new home and her new life.

"Sadie, darling, just relax and be yourself. Work in your beautiful gardens, shop, throw dinner parties, whatever makes you happy." They both discovered that she was an incredible artist. She painted in several mediums. J.M. encouraged her to live completely and fully, as a free, rich woman, in the fabulous city of New Orleans.

In no time at all, Sadie Beth was seen shopping at the exclusive dress shops in town, having lunch at the various tearooms, and entertaining in her lovely home. She became notorious for her gourmet meals, exquisite decorating skills, and playing the piano like an angel. Sadie Beth kept fresh flowers in crystal vases all over her home, from her garden during the growing season and from the local florists, otherwise. An instructor was hired to teach the new love of J.M.'s life to read, write, and count. J.M. wanted the whole world opened up to her. Money was deposited regularly in her name at several banks just for her use. Credit was established just for her all over town.

On one occasion, on the train ride back to Tennessee from New Orleans, J.M. had time to really contemplate what was actually going on in his life. It was tantamount for him to be respected and envied in Hawthorne and the surrounding communities. He must be feared by the slaves on his plantation or lose all control. These things have their rewards, but it simply wasn't enough. He now had the best of both worlds. Since taking on a hidden, forbidden life, he was still on top of his business as always. Everything was mighty good!

Never in his wildest dreams had Ferguson ever imagined the kind of total happiness he experienced with Sadie Beth. When in New Orleans with her, every evening after dinner, they would always go for a leisurely walk. They talked, laughed, and just enjoyed each other's company.

Every morning, they take their coffee out back and sat in the garden while listening to the birds, taking in the wonderful fragrances of the flowers, just enjoying nature, and each other. J.M. said to Sadie Beth, "This slower, simpler pace is heaven on earth. Some situations are bigger than life itself." Massa Ferguson was a well educated man, and being worldly smart, he very quickly figured out that at some point, maybe in the near future, or many, many years from now, this other life would have to be addressed. Right now, he simply wanted to bask in his newfound love and enjoy life.

Sadie Beth rubbed his shoulders, massaged his feet, and prepared his favorite meals. Ferguson was spoiled in ways that even he had never imagined. This special woman held his heart in her delicate hands.

Upon Massa Ferguson's arrival home, everything seemed normal as usual. Nothing ever really changed. His secrets were intact, but so were Miz Lucinda's and Annabelle's. Nothing was as it seemed.

After completing two days of inspecting everything at Tall Oaks and finding things in great shape (the crops, the livestock, the slaves), he thought to himself, *Now I can relax*. Leaving his horse at the barn and heading for the house, he said, "Must rule with an iron hand and stay on top of things."

Three large boxes had arrived while Massa Ferguson was finishing the inspections. Three slaves were trimming trees and working the flower beds in the back. Ferguson observed the boxes and asked the slaves to take the cargo inside to his study. He led the way. He then handed them tools, and, working carefully, showed them how to open the boxes. They took over and painstakingly opened and removed several pieces of fine imported French furniture. One slave named Lem said, "Massa, we kin do dat."

"Do what, boy?" replied Ferguson.

"Make dat nice funter."

"We show you Massa, come."

Out the back door, across the lawn, through the pin oaks, and to one of the slave shanties they went. "We do from dese." Lem said, holding up a stack of furniture catalogs.

"Dese be throwed out from de big house." Most of the pieces in the room were duplicates of pictures in the books, very good duplicates.

Ferguson sensed immediately this could be an incredible business venture. He gave Lem a sideways glance and said, "This is the beginning of something great.

"Boys, you have untapped abilities. We are going to put your talents to work."

Lem was an expert with the trees and flowers on the plantation but it did not generate the massa any money. His brilliant new idea had the potential to make him even richer.

After several weeks of contemplation and fact finding, Ferguson had Bo escort Lem and the other two workers into his den.

It was early, the sun had just come up. The three slaves were frightened. They had only been in the "big house" once before.

Massa Ferguson was sitting behind his big oak desk as they entered. They were greeted with "Come in, boys, sit down." In spite of the warm greeting, they were still afraid.

In his booming voice, Ferguson got right down to business. "Lem, Sam, Robert, in a few months all of you will be working inside a brand new building, making beautiful French furniture."

All the slaves were shocked! To work inside, out of the weather would be far better than they ever dreamed.

As the group departed to go back to their appointed duties, Lem lagged behind. "Massa Sir, kin I please give you some of my ideas on the work shop, Sir?"

"Why not, Lem. You and your friends will be doing the work."

"Thank you, Sir. I will make you proud," as he rushed to catch up with Sam and Robert.

Over the next several weeks, Lem and Massa Ferguson designed a three story building near the water's edge to take advantage of the cool breeze off the lake in the summer months. A stove was ordered for the cold months, the likes of which Lem and the other slaves had never seen. Lem was actually looking forward to the winter to enjoy the warmth from the new stove.

The new building had lots of windows that could be opened to provide cross ventilation and plenty of light to work by. Shutters were designed to lock over the windows when the shop was not in use. Needless to say, all the plans and construction was done by the talented slaves at Tall Oaks. The entire building was very open with stairs to the various areas of the plant. It was equipped with a block and tackle apparatus with padded pulleys to hoist the finished pieces to their proper places and not mar a single piece. Chairs, tables, chests all had their special place. It was a well run, organized operation. Of course, Ferguson did all the paperwork.

Once the work was underway, Ferguson contacted his brother in New York to help him find the best furniture finisher in the East.

Over the months, Lem had more than proven himself to be a leader and a visionary. Ferguson even left him in charge of his new project when he went back East to take the drawings, furniture finishes, and fabric samples. The orders were overwhelming. This new venture exceeded even Ferguson's expectations.

Needless to say, six months later, wagon loads of imitation French furniture was carefully packed and loaded, to be shipped down the Mississippi to stock stores all over the country.

This was the beginning of the first American made French furniture. It became very popular indeed. Every six months or so, another huge load was shipped to many large, high-end stores back East.

Ferguson was puzzled, to say the least. *How could savages from the jungles of Africa possess the ability to invent, build, and do all the things the slaves here at Tall Oaks were capable of.* It was only a fleeting thought from time to time, nothing important enough to waste time on. He just happened to be a shrewd business man with an eye for talented and trainable slaves. Luck was on his side.

For two long years, Miz Lucinda had taught Annabelle to read. And read she did—everything from children's books to the great books. This pleased Miz Lucinda highly. She had actually achieved something worthwhile since she got married.

Annabelle never neglected her work or devotion to the great mistress of the plantation. If anything, she worked even harder because she was so grateful. Once a month, Annabelle would carefully remove all the books and expensive glass pieces off the shelves in the library, treat the leather backed books, and clean and wax the shelves. She always lovingly dusted the expensive bric-a-brac. She always wanted the approval of Miz Lucinda once she put everything back.

Some time, during the day that she cleaned the book shelves, Annabelle always went to fetch Miz Lucinda. "Does it meet with your approval? Annabelle wants it to look pretty, but different every month."

"Oh, my!" Miz Lucinda would exclaim. "Every time you clean and rearrange the shelves, it is lovelier than the time before." She never realized that several books were always missing.

When the mistress was on a trip, it was an easy task to sneak books out to read and to teach from for her family. It was a bit more difficult when Miz Lucinda was home.

Over time, she and her family read every book in the Ferguson's extensive library. Reading was such a joy. Annabelle taught her husband and children every single night after they exercised. She used the very same techniques that were used to teach her. Dixon especially liked dictionary word books, and atlas books and maps. He learned to find Africa and America. He even studied the United States, so that he could find Tennessee. The children learned so much faster and easier than their parents, much to their parents' delight.

One night, after the lessons were finished, as likewise the reading out loud, Dixon said, "I swear to you, my wife and my beloved children, your learning will pay off. Trust me and trust in your Lord. Your mother and I have been pleading with our Father for a different and better life. It will happen." It had already been too long.

Both children smiled and said in unison, "We believe you, Daddy, and we love you." Annabelle knew in her heart that she had done a wonderful thing. Her entire family could now read.

Their next big hurdle was to gain their freedom, somehow.

Dixon was adamant about not being a slave. Every day of his life, he expressed his thoughts on the subject with his family. He knew that knowing how to read was a valuable tool. He and Annabelle both having viable skills was another. Now, to put all the pieces together and be free. Annabelle was not nearly as determined to be free as Dixon was. She worked in the big house all day. Miz Lucinda was very kind to her. She had complete freedom on the plantation. Dixon knew that there was more, much more to life, than being a slave.

Their children, Yancy and Dixiebelle, never got to play with other children in the evenings, never got to go to church on Sundays, or even attend any of the plantation social events that were held monthly. The children, along with their parents, did nothing in their free time but work, stay physically fit, and study to learn. It did not take long and the entire family was reading for pure pleasure. The four of them were very isolated and so very different from the other slaves. Only time would tell if it was worth it.

On several occasions, when Dixon and his family were reading in their shanty, they could hear the church service. It was always pretty lively and loud.

They would always stop what they were doing and listen to one of their favorite songs. "When we git to heaven we gwine sing, shout, and say, thank you, Lord, thank you, Lord, thank you, Lord. I love my peaceful new home. Never again will I need to roam, trying to find a happy home. I want to see his face, Lord take me out of this place. Thank you, Lord. I is free, I is free, I is free. You finally did send for me."

By the time the song was finished, Dixon's family was wiping tears from their eyes.

Every evening, as the slaves walked the quarter mile length of the tall pin oaks back to their shanties, the trees serve as a reminder of the separation on the plantation— the haves from the have-nots, the rich from the poor, the white from the black, the free from the slave. Behind the oaks lay a world of utter despair, work horses, human work horses with no voice, no respect, and no hope. The only way out was death. One day, not too far in the future, God was going to take notice and take action. Things will never be the same for the narcissistic, greedy plantation owner, and thieves and buzzards of human flesh. God does not like ugly, and this is ugly!

Chapter Eight

"The wheels grind slowly, but they grind very fine." One morning, up in that beautiful bedroom with the breathtaking Southern exposure, Annabelle was styling Miz Lucinda's hair as she had always done since shortly after she married the Massa and came to Tall Oaks. The day, thus far, seemed very ordinary. Miz Lucinda stared at Annabelle in the large ornate silver mirror in front of her and said, "I am now ready to present Mr. Ferguson with an heir to his throne. Why don't we both get pregnant? We can raise our babies together almost like one big happy family." Annabelle knew better, but said nothing. Plantation children were always sent off to private schools at seven or eight years of age until adulthood. They were never raised together beyond that age. They both agreed to stop taking their elixirs and became pregnant.

Miz Lucinda just knew this would strengthen her marriage, and Annabelle had no desire to be free or ever leave the plantation. A family cannot run with a baby. Annabelle's future would be secure.

Meanwhile, back in New Orleans, Sadie had just delivered the most beautiful and perfect baby girl anyone ever had. J.M. was delirious with happiness and pride. Their fate was sealed. Little Baby Beth Marie was the first heir to the Ferguson fortune. J.M. and Sadie Beth were more in love three years later than they ever were. He found her more fascinating than any other woman on earth. They were now a family.

Mr. Ferguson visited the Muse Plantation one last time. He bought Sadie Beth's mother and purchased her a home right next door to her daughter. That act of kindness made his Sadie so happy. It was the best gift he could have given her. He constantly looked for ways to make her happy. On the same visit, he brought her a set of ruby and diamond jewelry. "The rubies are for love, true love like we have. Diamonds are to show how rich you are." This loving couple had both, and a beautiful baby girl. Life could not have been better!

Sadie Beth looked up at J.M. and declared, "You are the most wonderful man in the world. I love you more than life itself. Because of you my life and even my mother's life is perfect. No woman on earth has ever known this kind of happiness."

"Honey, we both love each other more than life. I promise it will last forever."

J.M. had done everything he could to put Sadie Beth at ease. Now, they were both bound together by a beautiful daughter. "My heart is overflowing with pride and true love." He found that his life was better than he could have ever imagined.

When Ferguson was miles away, Sadie Beth and her mother worked in their flower gardens, or had breakfast at one or the other's home every single morning. They enjoyed little Beth Marie. They just enjoyed being free, privileged, and together. Life was incredibly wonderful for these two women. Of course, everyone thought Sadie's mother was her slave. They never told them any differently.

One of the slaves from the plantation nearest to Tall Oaks brought farm equipment, bridles, saddles, etc., that he needed help with. That was Dixon's job. The two men worked steadily all morning and talked and caught up with all the gossip. They discussed who had run off, who had got caught, who got away, etc. Dixon learned that there were rumors of a *civil war*. "What is a *civil war*?" Dixon inquired.

The other slave replied, "De Noth don't like de Soth for all the free work from us slaves. They is gittin rich off our backs. Up North, peoples gits paid fer their work." Even a slave knew more than Dixon, even if he couldn't read. The two worked and talked until quitting time that evening. The other slave headed home in the wagon piled high with all the repaired equipment he brought that morning. His Massa would pay Massa Ferguson. Dixon discussed the rumors of an impending war with Annabelle, and the fact that if the two of them were paid for their labor, inventions, etc., they would have money to live on their own. Just one problem: they had to get free or make it to the North. During a discussion with a slave from a nearby plantation, the subject of runaway slaves came up in addition to the impending Civil War. He told Dixon, "They done runned off and joined up with each other. They be killing plantation owners and they families, burn down the big house, burn the crops, and even kill the livestock. The last plantation weren't far from here."

These runaway slaves just live in the woods and do the best they can for food and a place out of the weather. They will do anything just to be free. While listening, Dixon thinks, *They will all be dead by spring. It gets cold in the winter in Tennessee.*

That night Dixon and Annabelle discussed the situation thoroughly. They conclude that the Massa should be told.

Early the next morning when Massa Ferguson entered the barn, Dixon and Yancy were feeding and grooming the horses. Dixon said, "Massa Sir, I needs to say something to you."

Dixon went into great detail about the possibility of an incident at Tall Oaks. Ferguson and Dixon set about making plans. It was understood that no matter what happened Mass Ferguson was to remain in the mansion with his family no matter what. Dixon volunteered to sleep outside by the dog run for the next several days until this all blew over. Bo and his helpers would be armed and not afraid to shoot to kill.

Dixon came up with the idea of bear traps located around the "big house" and the barns. The moment the first one snapped, Dixon would set the dogs free.

For almost a week, Massa Ferguson and Dixon travelled to several towns buying bear traps. Upon their return, they did not realize how lucky they were it had not taken them any longer.

The slave shanties were far enough from the main part of the plantation that they should be safe. It was the owners that were in danger. Annabelle and the children would be fine, Dixon assured them.

Every evening, the traps were set. Bo and his helpers were to take every third night on patrol. In the event anything happened, they were all on duty.

Only two nights after Tall Oaks plans were set in place, it happened. It was a dark, moonless night, about two o'clock in the morning on that memorable black night. The dogs had been barking and growling for the last twenty minutes. They had awakened Dixon. He was alert and ready for whatever was about to transpire.

All of a sudden, a trap snapped shut, then another. There were screams, then gunshots. The dogs had been set free, they were attacking the downed ones caught by the traps.

The defenders carefully made their way to one of the barns and got lanterns. They lit them to make sure they avoided the traps.

It seemed longer, but the battle only lasted about fifteen minutes. The grounds were littered with wounded and dead runaway slaves. It was a terrible shock that the plantation was prepared to successfully fend off their attack. Perhaps they will just keep running until winter stops them dead in their tracks.

After a while, Massa Ferguson stepped out on the back steps and yelled in his booming voice, "Is everyone all right?"

Bo replied, "All is clear, we are all accounted for."

With all the shooting, dog barking and loud commotion Miz Lucinda was totally unaware of what was going on just outside her home.

Every evening one of the downstairs maids would bring her a special sleep aide prepared by Annabelle.

The special elixir caused a deep restful sleep. In her nervous agitated state this was only the solution.

No one ever mentioned the frightening incident to Miz Lucinda. It would serve no wothwhile purpose.

In just one day everything was set right again at Tall Oaks. The bear traps were removed dead bodies were buried. Things were back to normal. The run away slaves were long gone.

"That is the worst thing that ever happened around here."

From that day on, Ferguson had a new respect for Dixon. They could have all been killed had it not been for Dixon. He thinks to himself, *He really is happy here, like I always thought. Why else would he alert me to such a dire incident.*

Day in and day out, year in and year out, nothing seemed to change when you are a slave on a plantation in the South. You work, you cry, you die. There were many changes in the air, but nothing tangible. Yet Dixon, being a very perceptive person and smarter than any common slave should be, knew an earth-shattering change was getting ready to happen. How he knew, only God knows.

When Annabelle told Dixon she was pregnant, he had mixed emotions, another one of their precious children being born into slavery. When will this nightmare end? His entire family could read, write, count, and possessed incredible reasoning power. They deserved to be free.

That very night, Dixon and Annabelle got on their knees and prayed for freedom and prosperity. This time, the heavens opened up and heard their fervent prayers.

One night, as J.M. and Miz Lucinda were preparing for bed, she excitedly hugged her husband's neck and announced that they were finally going to have a baby. J.M. froze! He could not breathe. He felt like he was going to faint. His beautiful perfect life was about to end. His mind was racing. He had to get a hold of himself. J.M. held his wife gently by her shoulders, looked into her eyes, and said, "Honey, this is unbelievable. I had long since given up on being a real family with children. This is a very special day in my life. You have made me a happy man!" What else could he say?

Hours later, J.M. lay awake in the dark, trying to clear his head. "How can a man have two families and love both of them, each in their own way?" J.M. just wanted to escape to New Orleans where he really didn't have to deal with anything but lighthearted happiness with the real love of his life, his soul mate.

The longer their relationship went on, the deeper their love and admiration for each other grew. How could a love this pure and deep be wrong?

Whenever Massa Ferguson was home at Tall Oaks, he made a real effort to act normal and be happy about Lucinda's pregnancy. This was not an easy task. After almost seven years of marriage, a baby! Anytime before J.M. fell in love with Sadie Beth, a family would have been fine. It was too late now! He had even gone as far as considering running away to New Orleans, taking half his money and his best slaves. He needed a new start. He already had a new life.

Back in New Orleans, he discussed in great detail how disappointed he was about the entire situation. On more than one occasion, he told Sadie Beth, "My heart is here, you and my child are here. This is where I want to be. Right now, I just feel trapped."

Massa Ferguson became more and more resentful. His beautiful wife was happy, glowing, and growing with child. Every day or so, she lovingly shows her husband all the tiny handmade clothing, knitted hats, and booties, and on and on and on. He thought, *Smile J.M. Say the right things, act interested.* What a bore! Even the slave women were busy making baby quilts, blankets, and even more clothing. Everyone was happy!

Everyone but Massa Ferguson. Ferguson started out being completely forthright with Sadie Beth, and he did not plan to stop now. Ferguson thought, *It is so wonderful to have someone you can lean on if need be. Life is not all that bad.*

Chapter Nine

Miz Lucinda was so happy preparing for the arrival of her first born. She really did not pay a lot of attention to how quiet and distant J.M. was, or even how much he was away from home. Each of them had their own agenda.

All the baby furniture was made right on the plantation, including the mattress. The nursery was perfect.

By late summer, both women were very pregnant. One day, Miz Lucinda asked Annabelle to make lemonade, put it on a tray with two glasses, and bring it down to the arbor. It was built right at the water's edge. Wisteria and honeysuckle grew over the top and shaded the area nicely. It was cool, quite, and peaceful, with the babbling brook rushing by.

When Annabelle arrived with the cold lemonade, Miz Lucinda said, "Sit awhile, Annabelle. No one can see that you are not working. It is very private here. My back is killing me and I do not work. You must be exhausted."

Annabelle sat down and poured each of them a glass of refreshing cold lemonade, and rested her aching body. She thought, *This has to be the life, you sleep till ten o'clock every morning, take a nap after lunch. How does it feel to never be tired?* Little did she know that one day, in the not-so-distant future, she would be rested, and not through death.

Annabelle had to remember above all else, slave or not, that Miz Lucinda was good to her and liked her as a human being. The little things mean so much when you were only a humble slave.

The two pregnant women, slave and owner, drank their lemonade, talked, rested, and enjoyed the peaceful reprieve. Miz Lucinda truly did understand. After about a half an hour, Annabelle stood up, took the tray with the pitcher and glasses, and headed back to the big house. She was grateful for just a short break from the mundane, never ending work.

Annabelle had been tired for years, but with the added burden of pregnancy, she ached until her body was encased in red hot blinding pain from sheer exhaustion.

A month before Annabelle's baby was due, her daughter, Dixiebelle, took over her duties, relieving her mother to rest up for childbirth. She needed very little training because she had helped in the house for several years. Annabelle was given time to rest before the birth of her child. Her capable hands would be needed with her mistress' new baby.

Annabelle rested, worked in her herb garden and gathered plants to dry, got baby things made, and rested some more.

Annabelle replied to Dixiebelle, "This is the life, to have time to spend with you and our family. This time alone justifies all the tiresomeness and pain. Miz Lucinda is a kind, understanding owner, not like all the others."

Dixiebelle's brow was creased. "Mama, remember what father has always said? Do not trust any white, nice or whatever." Annabelle had a puzzled look on her face, but said nothing.

"Mama, I must get back to the big house. Glad you enjoyed the lunch I prepared." And out the door she rushed.

Two weeks later, the circuit doctor delivered a tiny, perfect baby girl. They named their girl child, Pearl. They always referred to her as their "precious jewel." She was small-boned, sweet-natured, and almost never cried. The whole family thought of Pearl as their special gift from God. All thoughts of the "underground railroad" were forgotten. It was more than worth it when the family held precious Pearl, or when Annabelle held and nursed her. Life was not bad at Tall Oaks. Annabelle still had over a month to bond and take care of her little jewel before she had to return to work in the big house. Miz Lucinda was kind indeed.

Exactly two weeks after baby Pearl was born, the doctor delivered twin boys to Miz Lucinda, much to everyone's surprise. There had never been a more content new mother. From all outward appearances, everything seemed to be perfect. But things were far from perfect. Overnight, the contented new mother's milk dried up! The twins screamed from hunger. Their mother cried from frustration. Whatever would become of the hungry babies, Monroe and Jesse.

The very next morning, Annabelle was summoned to the Ferguson's nursery and told, not asked, to nurse the babies. With a baby at each breast, in just a little while, both babies were full, quiet, and sleepy. Annabelle was informed by Miz Lucinda that she had to nurse the babies and that her milk had dried up. "I do not want my babies drinking animal milk," the mistress of the house said. "There is plenty of goat's or cow's milk for your baby."

For two days, Annabelle tried unsuccessfully to save enough milk for her own child. The twins were hungry all the time. Miz Lucinda saw to it that her precious babies drank every ounce of milk Annabelle could produce!

Much to Annabelle's and Dixon's horror, baby Pearl was highly allergic to cow's and goat's milk. They both gave her the bloody flux. Several of the new slave mothers tried to nurse the baby, but to no avail. She knew her mother's touch, and the sweet taste of her milk. No one else would do. Starving to death made no difference!

Annabelle decided to appeal to Miz Lucinda on her baby's behalf.

Her answer was "I am truly sorry there is not sufficient milk to go around, Annabelle, but surely, you do understand," she said in her syrupy-sweet Southern voice.

The only thing Annabelle understood was that her baby was starving to death! How could a rational human being do such a horrible thing to a baby?

Baby Pearl's lips became parched. Her mother used lots of chipped ice and iced water from a spoon, but no milk. There just wasn't any left.

With a white baby at each breast, Annabelle watched helplessly as her baby whimpered, languished, and became a mere shadow of herself. Miz Lucinda never showed a glimmer of concern or sorrow, no interest whatsoever. Her well fed, healthy boys were thriving. She never allowed small incidents to worry her. What else on earth could even matter? All three babies were in the same room. Annabelle watched as death walked into the room and stole her little girl away. There was a hatred growing inside of Annabelle that was all consuming. What kind of devil could stand by and watch a helpless infant starve to death? Dixon had been right all along. The Fergusons were no different from any other slave owner in the south. They were all ruthless, evil, devil-possessed, narcissistic animals. Miz Ferguson witnessed this tragic incident and never even raised an eyebrow. The hatred inside Annabelle was palatable, bitter as gall.

The very last time Annabelle picked up her baby, she was limp. Her little arms and legs were thin and lifeless. Later that very night, precious baby Pearl peacefully quit breathing. Had any human ever felt this kind of pain? Breathing was difficult, happiness was gone forever. "How do you continue to live?" lamented Annabelle.

After the haze burned off the next morning, the day was clear, calm, and beautiful. Massa Ferguson walked into the barn and said, "Dixon, what are you doing, boy?"

Dixon replied, "I putting the last finishing touches on my baby girl's final resting box." Dixon was crying. His heart was broken, but not his resolve! Massa Ferguson did not even acknowledge Dixon's tears, the bitter tears of grief and hatred, hatred for the Fergusons.

A plantation funeral was always short. What was there to say? Each plantation had its own cemetery. There was very little to say about any slave. They were born, they worked, and they died. Some of them starved. Only one song was allowed. Baby Pearl's funeral was to be no different from any other slave's.

The morning of the funeral started off as usual. Annabelle groomed Miz Lucinda as if she were attending a grand ball. The twins were already fed for the next two hours.

Annabelle worked and waited to hear, *"I'm sorry,"* *"Too bad,"* anything. Not a word was uttered. The silence was maddening. As a result, the hatred burned inside her like red hot coals. How could she have been so stupid!

Dixon had warned her time and time again. It was now crystal clear why he was so passionate about being free.

The grave was dug, the casket was in place, and everyone assembled on either side of the grave. Bo, the overseer, and the Fergusons on one side, and Dixon and Annabelle, along with the plantation slaves, on the other side. The parents were numb from grief and sorrow.

Listening to the familiar field hands' hymn did nothing to comfort this bereaved couple or their two remaining children.

Throughout the entire funeral, Annabelle made several attempts to just make eye contact with the heartless, cruel creature from hell. She was standing there, holding her umbrella, looking at everyone except the grieving mother. In fact, she appeared restless, bored, far removed. All Annabelle wanted was a sympathetic glance in her direction. After all, it was Miz Ferguson's fault that her child was dead. Baby Pearl gave her life for Miz Lucinda's greedy boys. Did that not mean anything? As the casket was being lowered into the ground, Annabelle took one step forward, lifted her right hand toward the heavens, and spoke in a loud, chilling guttural voice in her native tongue. *"Mag die honde van hel, jou liggaam lewenoig vreet, van hier, insluituend jou nageslagtes, tot die ewigheid."* (May the hounds from hell feast on your live flesh and all future generations for an eternity!) There was a shocked silence over the group. No one, not even Dixon, had ever heard his wife revert to her African tongue. This quiet, peaceful slave had suddenly gone mad. Slowly, she slipped to the ground in a limp, exhausted heap.

In an instant, the sun went behind a cloud, and there was total darkness. A torrential rain ensued, drenching everyone, and filling the uncovered grave, causing the casket to bump from side to side. *Bump, Bump, Bump, Bump.* It was an ominous sound in the dark. Gradually, the sky became blue again and the rain ceased.

Annabelle's limp, wet body was carried up to the big house. This was ordered by Miz Lucinda. It was just about time to nurse the twins. Nothing stopped that indomitable rhythm that made up the whole of Tall Oaks Plantation. All in all, this day was different. The heavens opened up and heard Annabelle's humble cry!

For the better part of a year, Annabelle's tears flowed freely, and her shoulders were slumped. She had never experienced pain of this nature, a pain that kills your spirit, your soul, your every reason to keep breathing. Never again would she be fooled and used by anyone.

Until the death of her child and the way Miz Lucinda acted, or better yet, the way she did not react, Annabelle was blind and stupid. Until the twins were born, she actually thought she was a human being with dignity and a few rights. The weight of reality just about killed her.

The spell she casted never failed. All she had to do was wait. He may not come when you call Him, but He is always on time. Annabelle had renewed strength.

Chapter Ten

Months after the traumatic incident at the funeral of Annabelle and Dixon's baby girl, Pearl, things at Tall Oaks were different. Nothing you could put your finger on, but different. Their sadness permeated the air. The slaves appeared to be sleepwalking. They were very slow and deliberate. They were deadly quiet, even the children. They did not run, play, or laugh. There was no defiance, just absolute sadness and silence.

In the big house, things were different also. Annabelle did her work even better than ever before, moving quickly and efficiently, while the tears streamed from her sad eyes. There were no smiles, laughter, or friendly banter left in Annabelle. She was sad beyond reason. The fact that the twins were no longer nursing was such a relief. From that point forth, Annabelle never even glanced in their direction.

Miz Lucinda was fighting her own demons. First of all, why was her husband gone from home so much? Away on business? What kind of business? She was lonely. She felt like she was going mad. If it were not for her wonderful boys, she would just end it all. They were her only reason for living.

One evening, in her own shanty, Annabelle remarked to Dixon, "My husband, you were so right. These slave owners have no heart, no soul."

"Yes, dear, but just hold on a little while longer. It is all going to turn around. I can feel it in my spirit." Dixon held her hand, looked into her eyes, and smiled. "Just hang on and trust your husband, it is going to be all right for the four of us." Whatever would she do without Dixon? He was her strength.

As the months dragged on, Miz Lucinda gave up on even trying to talk to Annabelle, except to give strict orders or complain bitterly. That was just fine with her faithful servant. Nothing could ever hurt her again.

Two or three attempts were made to go shopping with Annabelle, but it was awful. How on earth could a person be present and so far away? It was crystal clear that her servant had devised a method to be present in her human form, only her mind and soul are far removed. Miz Ferguson thought, *This is absolutely embarrassing, even the clerks in the various stores noticed.* It was like not even having a personal slave servant. She would stare out the window when shopping with Miz Lucinda or simply wander off. How maddening!

On a rare occasion, when J.M. was home, Miz Lucinda broached the subject of Annabelle. "I sometimes feel that she hates me. She works harder than ever but she never smiles and only nods or grunts when I talk to her. If I did not know better I would swear she has been set free. She is no longer in awe of me. She hates me!"

"Now, now, honey, you have nothing to worry about. Maybe it is because her baby died. She is still upset. Just give her a little more time."

Lucinda knew full well, it was all her fault. She had committed a terrible injustice against Annabelle. Hopefully, time would heal all wounds.

Each night before retiring and each morning upon rising, Dixon and Annabelle prayed their prayer of faith. They both knew that their prayers were being heard and would be answered soon. This gave them great faith and patience. They were both determined to "keep hope alive."

Miz Lucinda watched Annabelle like a hawk. This person whom she thought she knew better than she knew herself had become a complete stranger. But in the transformation, she seemed more confident, very peaceful and calm, perhaps keeping a deep, dark secret. Much to Miz Ferguson's surprise, she had always thought that she and her husband's closest slaves were totally happy and devoted to them. How could she have been so naïve? She was suddenly struck with terror! If this was true, how safe was she and her family. There were some two hundred hostile unhappy slaves at Tall Oaks. There had been uprisings on other plantations, but could it ever happen here? The entire family could be in grave danger.

Night after night, Miz Lucinda had horrifying nightmares about being killed in her sleep, along with the entire family. The mansion, barns, fields, and everything were burned to the ground. The possibility of this happening was too horrifying to even imagine!

At one of her ladies' groups, there was a discussion about a Nat Turner, who led a slave uprising in which fifty-seven whites were killed by most of the slaves who were involved in the incident. At the time, she never gave it a second thought. The uprising slaves were slaves, but dangerous nevertheless. That was beginning to be quite apparent.

Massa Ferguson noticed his wife's agitation and lack of personal grooming. Annabelle had been banned from helping with Miz Lucinda's hair, wardrobe, or anything personal. "Inside, slaves are to clean and nothing else." Miz Ferguson was being eaten alive by her guilt. She had made a grievous mistake with Annabelle.

As the time dragged on, Miz Ferguson's disposition and appearance continued to get worse and worse. She was no longer that beautiful, tall, blond who was so carefree, vain, and totally happy. She had slowly turned to a real shrew. Her husband just shrugged. He had a wonderful life removed from this dismal household. Why ask questions? It really did not matter anyway.

J.M. was away from the plantation for longer periods at a time. She and the boys needed his protection. They would talk upon his arrival home.

Miz Ferguson had never been afraid in her life. Her parents loved her unconditionally. Her nannies spoiled her and always treated her like she was very special. She was courted and loved by an admiring husband. Fear was an unfamiliar emotion, but it had become a close companion.

There was even more talk about the rebel runaway slaves—Nat Turner, Denmark Vesey, Frederick Douglass, and many others. These rebels kept the happy, calm slaves upset and rebellious. They organized black groups all over the South, purportedly to kill plantation owners, burn barns and farms, write freedom papers, and set the slaves free. She and J.M. must address this dreadful subject.

Almost two weeks later, Massa Ferguson arrived home with toys and gifts for the boys, incredible fabrics, and even more fine diamond jewelry for his wife. J.M. and Lucinda talked at great length about runaway slaves, rebellions, and the rumors of an impending civil war. Not only had he gathered information in Tennessee, but all over the South. J.M. assured his wife that they had absolutely nothing to fear. Their wonderful lifestyle would go on forever. Slavery would go on forever. Massa Ferguson did hire two more men to assist Bo. Their jobs were to see and hear all. They were armed with guns and whips. There would be no rebellion at Tall Oaks. The three overseers were instructed to shoot to kill anybody if anything were to happen. This did little to assuage Miz Lucinda's fears.

J.M. said, "Not only did I tour the South on my last trip, I personally talked to Lincoln, our president. He assured me there would be no civil war and certainly no freeing of the slaves."

Lucinda smiled, "Do you really know the president?"

"I sure do, my love. The South will never fall. Now, let's go upstairs and forget all this foolishness." He wrapped his wife in his arm while walking up the stairs. "Do you like your gifts, you never said a word."

"Of course I like my gifts and I love my husband." *It was always so wonderful when J.M. was home,* she thought to herself.

Massa Ferguson was very kind and patient with his wife, not really understanding her fears at all. At this point in his marriage, they were direct opposites. He was light-hearted, easy going, happier than he had been in years. And oh, my, he even looked ten years younger. Miz Lucinda on the other hand had become old, cruel, worried, and mean. Where had that gay, happy, smiling witty, beautiful woman disappeared to? She simply was not young looking or young acting anymore. The twins were their mother's only delight. Jesse was dark headed and thick like his father. Monroe was fair skinned, blonde, taller than his brother, and thinner. Their mother loved them both equally.

Massa Ferguson had lots on his mind, but nothing showed on the surface. He had made up his mind to contact his barrister and redo his will. In the event something happened to him, he wanted his massive fortune split right down the middle for each of his two families. This would possibly turn out to be quite a shock for the true Mrs. Ferguson.

Ferguson, like many other slave owners, believed that the poor slaves were happy. All they needed to do was reverse the position and see how happy they were. None of the slave owners were as naïve about slavery as they pretend. George Mason, a slave owner himself, once said and believed, "Every master of slaves is born a petty tyrant. They bring the judgment of heaven on a country. As nations cannot be rewarded or punished in the next world, they must be in this. But an inevitable chain of causes and effects providence punishes national sins by national calamities. The threat of a Civil War certainly will bear this out."

Another slave owner, Thomas Jefferson said, "I tremble for my country when I reflect that God is just. His justice cannot sleep forever." A truer statement was never made!

Everyone in the South had a definite opinion about the war, rich and poor, slave owners or not. But so far absolutely nothing was being done. Dixon and Annabelle were sure something big was about to happen. Massa Ferguson had just returned home and was doing his usual head count and inspection when a messenger brought the news.

Fort Sumter in South Carolina has been fired on by the confederate soldiers, indicating that they wanted to succeed from the Union to decide for themselves. Their economy depended on free slave labor. What would become of the South without it? Many of the Southern states for several years wanted to be granted the rights to decide on slavery or not.

Chapter Eleven

Many spectators dressed in their party clothes, and went to the shoreline in North Carolina to cheer on the fighting. In the beginning, it was one big party, or so they thought. Everyone was so sure that the war would only last a few months. But little did they know.

By afternoon, everyone was exhausted, troops and partygoers alike. Bodies littered the ground and the earth was bloody and beginning to smell. About then fresh Southern troops arrived by train. That made the difference. They attacked with bloodcurdling shouts, called "The Rebel Yell." That was too much for the Yankees. They dropped their guns and fled.

The states wanted to form their own government that was founded upon one great truth—that the Negro is not equal to the white man. Therefore, they should remain slaves forever.

President Lincoln declared, "If I could save the Union without freeing the slaves, I would do so. What I do about slavery and the colored race, I do because it helps to save the nation." The Civil War raged on. It had been rumored before the war that the Southerners were lazy and could not fight because they were accustomed to their slaves doing the work. The Confederate soldiers fought like demons. Ralph Waldo Emerson felt that the government should pay the slave owners for their slaves and set them free. That would cost a lot less than going to war. If that first day at Fort Sumter was any indication, it was going to be a long, bloody war.

No one on earth was as surprised about the war as Massa Ferguson and Miz Ferguson. They talked late into the night about the ramifications of a Civil War. What would happen to them if the South lost? Neither of them knew anything but an affluent lifestyle. They had lots of free labor and loved being envied by their friends, business associates, neighbors, and almost anyone whose path they crossed. They were an awesome couple. Whatever would they do?

The victories went back and forth, never a really clear cut winner for very long. After two and a half years, Ulysses S. Grant and his troops were victorious over Chattanooga, Tennessee. There was the Siege of Vicksburg and the Battle of Gettysburg. Those victories gave Northerners hope that the war would soon be over.

As many as 135,000 Tennessee volunteers put on grey uniforms and fought for the Confederacy. Among this group were 20,000 African-Americans. More Civil War battles were fought in Tennessee than any other state, except Virginia. All together 454 battles and skirmishes were fought on Tennessee soil. Tennessee was the last state to succeed in 1864, The Battle of Nashville.

Slaves who lived near the North/South border fled their plantations and flooded military camps. Calling the run-aways "contraband," (property seized from the enemy), the

Union army protected them. An estimated half a million slaves claimed their freedom in this way.

"Damnation, damnation," declared Massa Ferguson. His empire was crumbling. "Those blasted Northerners hate us." He was fit to be tied. The trains were broken down because parts for repairs could not be shipped down the Mississippi River. It was blockaded. So were the towns and all the major roads. All he could do was hunker down with his family and hope this madness would soon be over.

On two different occasions, J.M. was able to wire money to Sadie Beth. He wrote, also. He asked her not to try to contact him. He would be in touch. *This is no way for a man to live*, he thought. Massa Ferguson talked to his wife and they both decided to send Dixon off to war. Miz Ferguson no longer got along with Annabelle, so as far as she was concerned, the whole family could leave. Miz Lucinda had made a grievous mistake with Annabelle and did not want to be reminded of what she did for the rest of her life.

Bo and Massa Ferguson took Dixon out a total of three times to shoot rabbits and squirrels. That was not much training to win a war.

On the morning that Dixon and his family were to leave the plantation, Massa Ferguson already had his banker, the barrister, and several leading business associates assembled in his large, impressive study. Ferguson's banker had located a small house with about half an acre of land for Annabelle and her children. There was plenty of room for a vegetable garden and to grow lots of herbs. *This is a dream come true*, thought Annabelle.

All the papers to free Dixon to fight in the Civil War for his freedom were on Massa Ferguson's oak desk. Dixon limped into the room with his head down, his spirit humble, and his heart racing. His time had come.

Massa Ferguson was settled in his high-back desk chair. The others assembled around the desk. Mr. Jefferson, the barrister, droned on and on with a lot of legal jargon. Then finally, Massa Ferguson said, "Dixon, sign right here. Put your X right here," pointing to the proper place to sign. Dixon limped over to the desk and started to scribble. He finished and slowly started to straighten up, threw his shoulders back, and took three steps backward, straight and tall. Ferguson inquired, "What did you write, what was all the scribbling, boy?" When he picked up the paper and read what Dixon had written, he turned white as a sheet. You could hear him for miles. "Well, damnation, a conspiracy has been perpetrated!" At that very instant, Ferguson did not know whether it was only Dixon who could write or whether the entire slave population of the plantation knew how also. Dixon had written perfectly, Mr. Dixon Ferguson. J.M. yelled, "Lucinda, bring me a glass of ice water." His right hand was over his heart. Was he about to have a heart attack?

Dixon, standing straight and tall, addressed Massa Ferguson and the rest of the group. He said, "Thank you all for your trust in me. I will do you and the South proud." He sounded exactly like the other educated men in the room. He clicked his heels and left the room without the slightest indication of a limp. Ferguson was too thunderstruck to even notice. What in tarnation was going on? An hour later, Dixon and his family departed Tall Oaks Plantation. Win or lose, once the war is over, Dixon is a free man because he fought for his country.

Chapter Twelve

It was August in the year of 1863. The United States was embroiled in Civil War—over two long years of bloody, brutal war.

There was a sergeant in charge of the company that Dixon was assigned to. He was not well trained or very informed about all the nuances of the war. Dixon was the only black in the group. The fifty or so other men were poor, illiterate farmers, and young boys, hardly old enough to shave, coming from all over the South. They had left wives and children behind while they fought for the South. At best, a meager living was the only thing these poor men could eke out, working from sunup till sundown. What would become of their families with them gone? Just one more painful thing for these pitiful soldiers to worry about.

In about a month, Dixon and the other troops were given lots of rations for their home base, along with writing paper to contact their loved ones back home. He wrote:

Dear Wife:
This miserable thing called war is a living hell. My platoon is as untrained as I am, but we must stay alive. Needless

to say, I am the only black I have seen since I became a soldier.

Please pray that this insanity is over soon. Hope that you and our children are doing far better than I am right now. Write when you can.

Your Husband,
Dixon

How in the world can you win a war with virtually no training, aside from having less food and very poor leadership? The few times Dixon went squirrel hunting did not make him a real soldier. He had never even fired, loaded, cleaned, or handled a gun until four weeks ago.

Dixon had always considered himself to be pretty savvy to have never been anything but a slave. Information was coming at him so fast that he could not begin to grasp it all. His very limited exposure, along with having no formal education made it extremely difficult.

One thing was for sure and certain, Dixon had to, no matter how difficult it may seem, stay alive, stay calm, and fight like the old devil himself had a hold of him.

The last thing Massa Ferguson said to Dixon before he left was, "Shoot and kill every damn Yankee in sight. The future of the South is in our Confederate fighting men's hands."

None of the men in his group had ever been exposed to a black man before, not even his sergeant. For months, it was very lonely, even scary. What was to prevent one of his fellow troops from gunning him down? Nature dictates that you kill or maim what you do not understand and possibly possessing a threat.

Slowly, ever so slowly, the men began to accept poor, scared Dixon. They discovered that he could read their letters from home and he could write letters for them. The men had taken it upon themselves to do things for Dixon, allowing him more time to read and write for them. The entire troop agreed that it was to their benefit to make sure he stayed alive. Every one of them needed him. That fact relieved Dixon immensely.

Dixon quickly learned that there were so many things in this new free world at this time of war that he did not understand. His entire life was, up to this point, spent working on a plantation, and driving his Massa around did not prepare him for real life or real war.

These people, these Confederate soldiers, were nothing like Massa Ferguson, his barrister, his banker, or any of the many guests who visited Tall Oaks. They were dumb, had no social skills, financial knowledge, or much of anything. The whole lot of them was downright pathetic, including Dixon, each in their own way. There were all black regiments in the war. Dixon entered too late to be sent to one or even leave the state. The war was hot and heavy by the time he enlisted.

Over and over in his mind, Dixon would wonder if the South was winning. Was the North winning? It was impossible for him to know. If winning had anything to do with being cold, hungry, scared, and being shot at each and every day, then maybe, just maybe, the South was winning. Fortunately, they had not of yet lost any men in the fighting in their little group.

Every day, Dixon repeated over and over "must keep hope alive, must keep hope alive. Some day very soon, I will be finished with this awful war, along with slavery. I will be as finished as a dead man is with breath." In his spirit, he knew that it could not be long from now. It was rapidly becoming more than he could deal with. This was not the freedom he had envisioned.

Reality really set in after about six weeks. The troops walked for miles through an aboveground graveyard. There were white, glistening, grinning skulls, and sun bleached bones everywhere. There were dead men and horses, frayed clothing that were still on some of the bones, and rusted guns strewn about. There was the putrid smell of death in the air. This had been a horrific battle with lots of lives lost on both sides. Onward they marched, no one had time to figure out who had won or who had lost, and they were just looking for Union soldiers to kill.

Nothing in this world had upset Dixon more than that horrific sight. His whole body shook like a leaf on a tree in a windstorm. Dixon actually felt like someone had dropped an old dirty wet wool rug over his entire body.

Sergeant Brown yelled, "Buck up, men! This is war! Get used to it, okay. Now march!" This was no place for pantywaists. Dixon quickly figured that out.

They had to go around the battlefield. There was not room enough to even put a foot down without stepping on a body.

Much later, Dixon found out that was the Battle of Franklin. Some fifteen hundred soldiers, mostly Confederates, were killed. After that sobering experience that night, as Dixon lay under his blanket on the cold hard ground, he began to reflect on some very dark thoughts he had but refused to address. To the best of his limited knowledge, up to this point, being free was far more awful than being a slave. For months, he had endured some terrible things—shooting, stabbing fellow human beings—simply because they did not agree with others beliefs concerning the nation. When will the killing end? Is being free mainly about death and war? What about sleeping in the woods? It's either so cold you wish for death or so hot you have trouble breathing.

April 1864, the rains came down for weeks. Like a cow pissing on a flat rock, there was no end to it. You had to eat in the rain, crawl on your belly in the rain, fight in the rain and mud. Was anything besides death and bloodshed being accomplished? His brain and soul both felt like they were being attacked by a swarm of bees. There was nothing but pain and uncertainly.

Every day now, Dixon repeated over and over again, "Must keep hope alive, and someday soon, I will be finished with this awful war and hellish slavery, as finished as a dead man is with breath." In his heart and soul, he knew it could not be long now. "God is still on the throne."

In all his living days, Dixon had never been hungry, but lately, he had eaten rats, snakes, and stolen chickens from poor farmers along his war journey. Just the thought of it made him weak and sad. The men in his unit were in no way as well off as Dixon had been on the plantation. What is this so-called "freedom"?

Every day of his now miserable life, Dixon had his doubts about being free. His beloved Annabelle was much smarter than him. "Must keep hope alive" became his mantra.

It wasn't often that Dixon got to write home, but was glad when he could. He wrote:

My Beloved Wife:

How are things with you and our children? I surely hope everything is well with my family. We agreed to enroll Yancy in school this fall. Let's enroll Dixiebelle, too. A girl child needs all the education she can get. Free blacks must be smart and educated.

Tell everyone back home howdy. Sure hope this damnation of a war is over soon. My sergeant is bringing you some money. Please be ever mindful what we are doing with our money. How is your "herbal business" doing? Pretty well I hope. Hug the children for me and I love you all. God Bless
   —Dixon Ferguson

Some weeks later, Annabelle Ferguson wrote back to Dixon:

My Dear Husband:
   Things are going better here than I can truly comprehend. There has been a surge of illnesses. I can hardly keep up with the demands put upon me. Medical supplies cannot get through. All the roads, towns, and even the Mississippi are all blockaded. I am supplying the circuit doctor and the chemist with my elixirs for all manner of cures. The money is pouring in. Our plans are actually coming together just like you said they would. Both children are in school. They are happy, healthy and learning a lot. We miss you and send our love and respect to you.

Your loving wife,
Annabelle Ferguson

Chapter Thirteen

It was years before Dixon learned about the many battles, generals, etc., in the Civil War he fought in. As he was serving, the bad news continued to get worse about the war. The Battle of Shiloh shocked the nation. In this one conflict, more soldiers were killed than in all three wars that had been fought on American soil before that day (The Revolutionary War, The War of 1812, and the Mexican-American War) combined. The battle lasted for two days, resulting in the defeat of the Confederate Army. There was so much bloodshed in Tennessee that a lot of the streams and rivers ran red with human blood. War along with slavery is truly hell on earth.

In the end, more than fifteen percent of the soldiers on the front lines were black. The blood of the black and white men flowed freely together for the *Great Cause*, which was to give freedom.

Meanwhile, the Fergusons at Tall Oaks had their share of problems. The slaves that had not run off, Miz Lucinda, and the twins were all in an underground storage house. The Yankee soldiers burned crops and looted the mansion of sterling silver and other valuables for several days. Their horses defecated on the floors and expensive rugs and broke the magnificent hand-carved mahogany banister down completely. Ornate mirrors were broken, horses and cattle were set free, fields burned, and then they left. Several weeks later, it happened again, and then a third time. There was very little at Tall Oaks to be proud of anymore.

About a dozen of the older slaves remained. The younger ones and their children had long since run off, joined the Confederates, gone North, or just disappeared. J. M. and his wife were mortified. "What in tarnation kind of war is this!" exploded Ferguson. "Those damn Yankee soldiers destroy everything in their path." They found themselves helpless and hopeless. The few old, worn down slaves left could not begin to set this place right again.

Due to Ferguson's ignorance at that time, he still thought he was a very rich man. All he had to do was buy more slaves. In a matter of months, things would be even better than before. It had never occurred to Ferguson or any of his brilliant peers that if the South loses the war, their money would be worthless. The wealthy South would fall.

It had been months since J.M. was able to contact Sadie Beth. The waterways, roads, and towns were blockaded because of the war. The trains were all broken down. Repair parts could not get through. Sadie was given strict orders to never contact him. He paid her accounts and kept money in the bank for her use. At least, he did not abandon her.

Massa Ferguson's whole world was in shambles. There was no contact from the outside world. No one had been by in weeks. Where were his friends that had visited frequently? The Ferguson's buggy and coach had been both destroyed. They were chopped up and burned. All his prized horses were set free, some were even shot. He was stranded at Tall Oaks.

Finally, about three weeks later, word got to J.M.'s plantation that the war was over! The South had lost! Even worse news was that the slaves were free. Something called the "Emancipation Proclamation" handed down by President Lincoln stated, "On the first day of January, A.D. 1863 all persons held as slaves within any state or designated part of a state, the people whereof shall be in rebellion against the United States shall be then, henceforward and forever free." Massa Ferguson no more, just plain Jesse Monroe Ferguson. That same fateful day, much to his disbelief, he discovered that his money was worthless. Taxes were due on his mansion and the land. What in tarnation was a formerly rich and powerful man to do? These were precarious times!

Miz Ferguson just took to her sick bed. How in heaven's name does one live without money, land, and slaves? Her life was over. Her parents were in the same awful fix. They owned a tobacco plantation in Alabama.

Miz Ferguson's bedroom no longer has the beautiful pale blue silk draperies and matching coverlet. They had been torn down and destroyed. If she just kept her eyes closed, she could not see the ravages of war inflicted upon her life and her beloved home.

Dixon was a free man at last! The war was over! Lincoln freed the slaves. Dixon won his freedom twofold— he fought in the Civil War and Lincoln freed him. He was free indeed.

Although he was a little over a hundred miles from home, it took over a week by foot to make the trip. Blacks were everywhere, celebrating their hard fought freedom from slavery and the Civil War. They called it a "Jubilee."

They sang and danced for days. They were free and jubilant. Nothing short of dying and going to heaven could even come close to this momentous occasion. With no slaves to tend the plantation, they would surely go to ruin.

There were women, men, and children, along with cows, oxen, horses, and chickens in cages. Everyone was singing and dancing. Dixon had heard the same song for miles so he began to sing. "It is a jubilee, jubilee. They done set the slaves free. My heart is filled with glee. Dat man Lincoln made us equal to any man. Made us free in his own land. Jubilee, jubilee, jubilee. My tired body and soul are now free. We gwine dance, sing, and have a jubilee."

Dixon was so overcome with joy that he began to do back-over flips down the dusty road.

It was mind-boggling; the thousands of ex-slaves that Dixon encountered on his trip back home. Some were already headed North, while others at the moment had no place to go but back to their respective plantations. They were in dire need of direction. Many of them needed to reunite with their loved ones. They had been sold to other plantation owners.

It was dusk dark when Dixon arrived at the house his family had moved to when he went off to war. Even in the little daylight left, he could see that many improvements had been made to the modest house and the land surrounding it. The house had been painted off-white with green shutters. The steps had been repaired and flowers were blooming everywhere. He could hardly wait to view the sides and back in the daylight. The whole family greeted him with hugs, laughter, and tears. They were altogether happy, healthy, and free! Their every prayer had been answered.

They got to bed late, but early the next morning, they were up having breakfast together before sunrise. Dixon could not praise his wife and children enough for what they had accomplished around their home. It was amazing! The place was wonderful! Annabelle had a large vegetable garden, watermelon patch, and herbs enough to supply the entire county. The biggest surprise was still to come.

For two days, Dixon and Annabelle talked and made plans. She explained in great detail the ratification of the "Emancipation Proclamation" for fear that it would only stand as long as Lincoln was in office. It became the Thirteenth and Fourteenth Amendments to the Constitution, making slaves free forever. Annabelle had access to newspapers and read them from front to back every single day. Dixon was so proud of his wife.

When they finally got around to it, Annabelle revealed just how much money they had amassed. Every penny she got her hands on, she bought gold. When a patient could not pay, she accepted payment in chickens, pigs, cows, and what have you. She and Yancy immediately sold whatever it was and bought gold. She became the local doctor and pharmacologist. In actuality, that was harder than working on the plantation. The children helped a lot. The fortune his wife and children had saved was shocking. Dixon said, "Honey, we are on our way. Most white Southerners are penniless and all the newly freed slaves are, too. The fact that we have money can open a lot of doors!"

Chapter Fourteen

Dixon and Annabelle agreed that he should visit Massa Ferguson at Tall Oaks one last time. They both felt it was the right thing to do.

Early the next morning, Dixon saddled Yancy's horse and headed the short distance south. The first thing that caught his attention was the fact the fences were torn down and crops had been burned. He did not see or hear a cow, horse, chicken, or anything. There was a depressing feeling in the air. As he went up the meandering brick paved path to what used to be a beautiful white mansion, he saw that the brush was overgrown and the flowers were dead. He thought, *Oh, my, the lack of free labor. Oh, well, what price for freedom.*

He dismounted, hitched his horse, and walked up the front steps. This was a first. After knocking several times, an old black woman answered the door. She was formerly a field hand at Tall Oaks. She reasoned that she had no place to go so she stayed on. She was too old to be much good to anyone. The old woman shuffled off to fetch Massa Ferguson.

In a few minutes, they stood face to face. They were now two free men, one black, one white, one rich, one penniless. "Well, Dixon, it is good to see you. How are things going?" asked J.M.

Dixon responded, "Very well, Sir, how about you?"

"That dad burned war ruined me, not in a thousand years did it ever occur to me that the South could possibly lose the war. My money is worthless, my slaves are gone, and taxes are due on my house and land. Miz Ferguson is heartsick. She never leaves her room!" replied J.M. "As you can see, those Union soldiers tried to destroy this place. They used the downstairs as a barn for their horses. I do not think the urine and shit smell will ever go away! They used the cellar for a mortuary as it was the coolest place to keep the corpses until they could bury them. That hand-carved banister was ripped down by those idiots. Why can they not fight wars on the battlefields? With no money and no slaves, this place can never be restored," bemoaned J.M.

Dixon stood straight and tall, looked Ferguson in the eye and said, "How much are the taxes, Sir?"

J.M. walked over to his desk in the study and picked up the bill and handed it to Dixon.

"Sir, I am prepared to pay the taxes and give you traveling money. Everything is to be left as is. You take nothing."

Ferguson was flabbergasted. He blustered around, cursing under his breath. Finally, he said, "You have a deal!"

Dixon replied, "You are to be out in two weeks, taking nothing but yours and the family's clothes. The barrister will draw up the papers and we will finalize the deal in his office. I will fetch you at 9:00 A.M. on Thursday in two weeks to complete our business," advised Dixon.

Dixon's speech and actions were swift and decisive. At this point, the only thing J.M. could do was follow Dixon's directions. His wonderful life had become a living nightmare. Surely, he would not be taking orders from former slaves for the rest of his now miserable life. He would rather be dead! Even hell would be better than this!

Things could not be worse. Miz Lucinda did not in any way resemble the dignified, refined, beautiful former mistress of the manor. She was stoop shouldered, disheveled, and her eyes had a vacant far away stare. She shuffled when she walked. Of course, she showed no recognition of Dixon.

On his short ride home, he had an epiphany—he would now be the king on the throne, and Annabelle, his queen. His children would be heirs to the throne.

Later that evening, when Annabelle returned from her rounds and the children returned home from school, he told them the good news. They were stunned. Could this be a dream? Annabelle was speechless. She had always believed in her husband and was not going to stop now.

Two weeks later, Ferguson and his family left town on one of the few trains that had been repaired, bound for New York. They took nothing but their clothes and personal belongings. J.M. had a brother there in the shoe manufacturing business. He left to work for him. Ferguson no longer wanted to live anywhere in the South. There were too many memories.

Neither time nor money permitted him to see Sadie Beth one last time. For this he was truly sorry.

A slave named Hannibal Foster did a lot of wrought iron work at Sadie Beth's house. His Massa hired him out to work all over New Orleans. There was none better. That was why Ferguson hired him.

One month after obtaining his freedom and procuring a paying job, Hannibal came to call on Sadie Beth. He had flowers in one hand, his hat and heart in the other. He explained to Sadie that he was aware of her past and it did not matter. It was love at first sight for both of them.

Three months later, they were married in a private ceremony in her home. It was a fine union indeed. Sadie Beth owned the home and all the finery. Hannibal earned the money to continue her lifestyle and certainly better his.

They were a beautiful couple. He was tall, strong, handsome and also a mulatto. His new wife patiently taught him to read and do math. He learned to figure his jobs correctly. With her help, they both did great and were unbelievably content.

Dixon and his family moved to Tall Oaks. The first thing he did was hire a cook, a maid, and several field hands. The help all lived in the quarters behind the mansion. The field hands were paid small wages and a handsome percentage when the profits come in. There was also a full-time gardener. The furniture makers returned, and Dixon worked out a very fair deal for them and himself. Tall Oaks was once again a booming, profitable place.

Slowly, ever so slowly, Tall Oaks became more beautiful than it was even in the past. The workers were happy, well paid, and free. The Dixon Fergusons were rich, happy, and free.

Even before the work was firmly underway, their children were sent to private boarding schools back East. Education was so important for Yancy and Dixiebelle.

Annabelle felt like a very young woman again. She only had to give instructions to the household help: do beautiful hand work, play cards, and enjoy her new life. Dixon treated her like the beautiful, fragile piece of glass his wife used to carefully clean. That was a lifetime ago. She was never to do hard labor again. Their lives were even better than they prayed or dared to dream for.

Two years later, Dixon built a school on his property. The school was for his hired hand's children and anyone else in the area who wanted to go. The state paid the teachers, and he and his wife did the rest. Education was so important! He and Annabelle were living proof.

The years passed, J.M.'s passion for Sadie Beth waned, and money was tight. What could he do? He was a broken, lonely old man.

Every Saturday morning, Dixon and Annabelle would go to town in their fancy carriage with their own driver. They ran errands and went to the post office. That particular morning, there was a very special piece of mail for them, just six short years after the Civil War. It was an invitation to the governor's ball.

On the evening of the ball, Dixon and Annabelle could hardly contain their delight. Dixon was dressed in a black frock coat with hand-carved ivory buttons down the front of his white formal shirt. Annabelle wore a pale gold French gown. She was adorned with magnificent diamond jewelry. She felt like a queen. No one but Dixon and Annabelle ever knew about the treasures that were left behind by Miz Lucinda in her bed posts. Untold amounts of gold and jewelry were completely forgotten about by Miz Lucinda in her feeble state. This greatly assisted Dixon and Annabelle in achieving their dream of reconstructing Tall Oaks to its original glory.

This was truly a special event, yet another milestone in their lives. To be invited to the governor's ball personified that you had truly arrived. They were a viable part of Tennessee society. Nothing could have pleased them more.

Their lives were rich and full. The children were away at boarding school. They wrote letters; needing money, typical rich kids. The following is a good example:

My son, Yancy:
Sure hope you are learning a lot and having a good time. Have you made many new friends? I sure hope so. Things here at Tall Oaks are going well. I have never in my whole life worked so hard or been so happy. When it is yours, you work and never get tired. Enclosed you will find a check to cover your trip to Europe. Spend it wisely, be careful, but do have fun. I look forward to hearing all about your new adventure.
Your adoring father,
Dixon Ferguson

My Darling Dixiebelle:
How are your studies coming along? Are the teachers understanding and patient? Whatever am I thinking? You are probably teaching some of the classes by now (smile). Enclosed you will find a check to cover your going shopping with your new girl friends. Hope you find lots of pretty things. Tall Oaks is coming into its own more and more every day. Your father is a happy man. I cannot wait for you to see for yourself.
Your proud and loving mother,
Annabelle Ferguson

The years passed and Yancy graduated with honors from Georgetown with a law degree. Yancy and his father decided he needed to be a barrister to help keep the family holdings in perfect order. In time, Dixiebelle graduated from medical school and set up practice in New York City. She was a natural. Her specialty was surgery, heart surgery in particular.

This family was able to "keep hope alive" and achieve their fondest dreams. Their legacy would live on through the generations.